**Also by J.C. Ellefson**

*Foreign Tales of Exemplum and Woe*

*Under the Influence: Shoutin' Out to Walt*

# Conversations with the Underground

J. C. Ellefson

Fomite
Burlington VT

This book is dedicated to my grandchildren, Spencer Archer Smith, Roger Mason James Smith, and the very new-to-this-world, Victoriosa Imelda Leora Aguado Wright-Neil Sierra. *Este libro está dedicado a mis nietos: Spencer Archer Smith, Roger Mason James Smith y —recién-lle-gad-a-este-mundo— Victoriosa Imelda Leora Aguado Wright-Neil Sierra.*

In the years ahead, if you ever need some backup, you'll be able to find me in these pages. *En los años venideros, si alguna vez necesitas apoyo, podrás encontrarme en estas páginas.*

# Contents

# Overture

We're on the cusp of summer in Vermont, which can mean only one thing for sure: the numbers are getting bigger, and it has nothing to do with predictable weather. A couple of days ago, it was in the high 30s. Three weeks ago, there was a hard frost, and it took out our pear and cherry blossoms. Tomorrow, it's supposed to be in the 90s. In a few days, we'll see 40s again.

Nothing's for sure around here except the people. When I was young, I never realized that writing was a team sport. Here's my team. Here are the people who have helped me write this book.

Thank you, Marc Estrin. Yes. You might be disembodied, but you continue to be a brilliant editor and mentor. Nancy Means Wright, you're part of the Disembodied Poets, too, but your light shines on. You're still my biggest fan. We continue to walk in your footsteps. Jim McRae, thanks for taking time away from the dogs and sheep to read and comment on my work. It's a treasure. Champion author and coach, Gary Wright, your motto "If it is to be, it is up to me," does more than win hockey games. Marty Burgess, many thanks. You are a one-of-a-kind stellar technical advisor, sounding board, and friend.  Thank you, Erik Neil. If writers really understood that your editorial skills are nothing short of magical, they would be camping at your doorstep at the Purple Crow Farm. Savant carpenters Adam Heath and Bill Casavant, thank you for also showing us all what gifted story-telling is all about. The Trustees of Champlain College, I need to thank you for my last sabbatical. I felt like I was Federico García Lorca. I was able to work on this book—and my forthcoming novel--while walking through Spain—but unlike Lorca, I was let live. It has been the experience of a lifetime collaborating with you, John Rasmussen. Your filmmaking is nothing short of genius and your camaraderie--a rare gem. Tal Birdsey, thanks for teaming up with me. We're going to charge—with our books in hand—straight into the barricades. Donna Bister, you are an extraordinary person carrying Fomite Press on your shoulders. You're our Lighthouse. You show everyone what it takes to bring books into the world, and the books you make are works of art in their own right. Yes, by all means, judge *Conversations* by its cover and layout. If so, I'll receive a Nobel, plus the Pulitzer. Lesley Wright, my partner here at Summer's Gale Farm, there is too much to say. Yes, sometimes the water gets choppy trying to keep the roof on, trying to keep the animals fat and happy--and on this side of the dirt. You're an indomitable force, and I reap the benefits. Your world is writing, words, and literature, along with black dirt, seeds, brown-pants grandchildren, ancient six-toed cats, and I reap the benefits. I don't have to do the math. I know it all adds up to paradise.

I hear an early morning boom of thunder to the west. Not in the forecast. Does a weather predictor lie more than the current sitting president? And now, here comes the rain and hail. Answer: nowhere close.

Summer's Gale Farm, Leicester, VT—on the cusp of summer, 2026.

Many thanks to the editors of publications where some of these pieces first appeared: *American Indian Culture and Research Journal:* "Apache Tears"; "Star of the American Road"

*College English*: "For Pete's Sake" ; "On the Brink of Leaving Holiday Town"

*Contemporary Review*: "Chilling Out in the Lincoln Avenue Cemetery"

*Crab Creek Review*: "The Blacksmith's Dog Story"

*Crickett:* "The Strange Disappearance of Peter January. . . "

*Embers*: "The Way It Is Deep in the Frozen Lake"

*Fine Madness*: "Strolling Dark Town with Mother"

*Mr. Cogito*: "Trying to Imagine Norman"

*Nimrod*: "Celebrating Gary Snyder's Birthday. . ."

*Paris/Atlantic*: "Who I Am and What I Want to Know"

*Renegade:* "Self-Portrait with Straw Hat

# underground

: a movement or group organized in strict secrecy among citizens especially in an occupied country for maintaining communications, popular solidarity, and concerted resistive action pending liberation.


"A kingdom underground. . . is always a place of strangely fluid and polymorphous beings, unimaginable torments, superhuman deeds, and impossible delight."

—Joseph Campbell

## Under the Spell of the Light

"You can learn from ancestors in all their forms. Because
the dead  control the past, they control the stories. . ."
—Margaret Atwood

In the firelight, my mother is smiling, my brother, too. All of us are smiling. The
hot chocolate is so hot that it could burn right down your throat and empty out
through all of your toes. The idea is that hot chocolate keeps us warm on the
inside, and the fire keeps us warm on the outside, not to mention the feast that my
mother has hanging in our eighteenth century fireplace. We have enough beans for
a hockey team hanging from the crane; three Cornish game hens on the rotisserie
spit; steamed kale and brussel sprouts from the garden; Ball Park foot long hot dogs
on sticks—my brother's input—cornbread in the beehive oven; and a Dutch oven
full of cherry cobbler nesting in the coals.

The chairs, however, are my father's black plastic, sticky Danish modern inside-
of-a-Bergman movie uncomfortable pieces of abomination. Apparently, one of their
first page agreements as newly weds was that my father would acquiesce to living
in her drafty eighteenth century French manor house on the coast of No-where,
Maine, if he could choose the furniture. She readily agreed, stored all her French
museum-quality pieces carefully in the attic, and saw a unique union of the old and
the new, which can show us all just how blind love is. She never saw the hair-trigger
temper, the petulant bullying , or the 100 proof black eyes that came with him. All
that was tucked away somewhere in the appendix in fine print.

"That's why those Danish Vikings were always raiding," I say. "I'd fight my way through Europe, too, if this was the only thing I had to sit on."

Both of them laugh, my brother shaking his head, saying something like maybe the Scandinavian old man would return from his latest European business trip with a long ship full of comfortable furniture.

"The problem is that he's already shown up with a long ship full of this junk. Which country has over-stuffed chairs, and is Big Fat Bob going to bring back any of those?" I ask.

My mother feigns contemplation, looking up at the cracked, sagging horse-hair plaster ceiling, raises a finger to her lips, and puts on her fifth grade teacher's voice.

"Boys, which countries in Europe are known for their innovations, comfort, and design?"

My brother chuckles to himself.

"Well, perhaps we can narrow it down this way. We already know which country is famous for everyday domestic torture."

My mother does her dragon laugh, the one that blows mirth from somewhere deep in her chest, but my brother keeps on his business face, which is as close to terrifying as you can get at fifteen. Since little league, he has been studying the faces of the great pitchers and has already settled on something completely his own. He can now scowl, ignore, and mock a batter all at the same time. At fifteen, he's a phenom. He's a 6'3" brown-haired bean pole. He can launch himself over the bar in the high jump like Barysnikov, and he can throw an 85 mph fastball on the corners right past your knees. I think most kids can't even see the ball. Most of the time, when kids swing, the ball is already in the catcher's mitt. In the firelight, I see his red Stanford University sweatshirt hanging like a blanket over his chicken wing shoulders. The coach at Stanford showed up at one of his games laden with collegiate paraphernalia and free-ride scholarship talk, and that coach wasn't alone. The entire sports community of our town keeps wondering how fast Jake is going to throw when he fills out, which pro team he'll play for, and whether or not he'll forget all his old friends in terms of tickets once he arrives in the Bigs, but none of this is ever going to happen. In a couple of years, Jake will find his own way to die years before his time, but right now, he's still ours, vibrating in the firelight.

My mother doesn't give up.

"So, which countries?"

A gust of wind throws freezing rain hard up against the diamond glass windows that my mother's Great Great Great Great-Grandfather Spencer brought back from Normandy during the French Revolution. My mother throws her head back and laughs.

For three days now, everyone on the coast has been preparing for Iceageddon, what Wally Kinnan the Weather Man has been calling our storm of the century. The prediction is for widespread power outages up and down the east coast. Transportation will come to a standstill. 'Expect major hazards of falling electric lines, downed trees, collapsing roofs and bridges. Don't leave the safety of your home if you don't have to. Travel may be limited to ice skating only,' reported Wally, whose sense of humor is a little like licking an unsalted saltine. "Folks, during Iceageddon, we'll be living the lives of our eighteenth century ancestors. On Sunday afternoon the 40 degree day will plummet to 28 within two hours, and the two inches of rain predicted will hit the cold ground as ice the like we've never seen before."

My mother's cheeks flush at the news. She slowly raises her eyes upward with her palms together in prayer.

"Thank you, O Lord God Baby Jesus for some dramatic weather. I thought I was going to lose my mind if we had another fucking beautiful day."

Both my brother and I double over. It's not the irony that she was everybody's favorite fifth grade teacher who swore like a mariner at home. Home front profanity was a part of her art form. Sometimes her words would escape her mouth with the color of Van Gogh's *Sunflowers*. Sometimes her words were sculpted and held your heart. She might have given Michelangelo a pep talk before he raised a chisel to the *Pieta*. Even as a kid, I was grateful that such power never fell into the wrong hands.

Along with world geography, mathematics, music, and great literature, my mother also instructed us in swearing, early and often. When I was in third grade, when she heard me call my brother a 'dirty bum', she made both of us take a knee—like we were on her class baseball team.

"Now, Jim, if a person who identifies as a male crosses you or does you a disservice in some way, call that person a bastard, and if that person falls in the female camp, you call that person a bitch, loud and clear. Do you understand?"

I nodded.

"Now, try it again."

I turned to my brother, who was five years my senior. I pointed my finger at him and shouted it out of my eight year old lungs.

"Jake, you're a dirty, dirty bastard."

My mother stared at us for a good three seconds before giving her curt nod. I imagined her in front of a chalkboard, pointer in hand with an audience of thirty-five kids, all straight-spined with folded hands on their carved graffitied desks. You'd get the same curt nod if you raised your hand and told her that the capital of Uruguay is Montevideo.

"Next time, we'll talk about time and place. Context, boys, is everything. For now, don't swear away from home. Think about profanity like you're building a sandwich: throw in some mustard, try it on rye, secret sauce, greens, a little provolone. In the near future, we'll also work on swearing in foreign languages. Your worlds will become larger, and doors everywhere will inexplicably open for you. Now, go outside."

I spent the entire afternoon shouting bitch and bastard into the wind, adding condiments. By the end of the afternoon, I had come up with 'why you razzle-dazzle baby puke yellow limping monkey bastard.'

Profanity was my mother's great Italianate royal blue cashmere trench coat, but dramatic weather was part of her DNA. Her only worry about Iceageddon was that Wally Kinnan the Weatherman would get it wrong.

"Finally boys, we're receiving some good news, but we need to mobilize."

We mobilize. By Sunday morning, we have Great Great Great Great's French oil lamps down from their attic bardo, positioned strategically throughout the house, filled, wicks trimmed, and ready to light. We have wheel-barrowed about three cords of nicely split oak and maple into our barn, which is attached to our house through a series of connecting sheds, and the weight of canned goods in the larder is making the wide French shelves sag. Somewhere in the vast attic, my mother finds an ancient, slightly balding, coonskin cap of one of our ancestors, which she proudly presents to me, along with some mouse compromised leather hunting boots, and a hand-made antler-handled ten inch sheath knife with a broken point, just in case I get 'separated from the group.' For the next three days, I wear the coonskin cap to bed.

By 2:00 P.M. Sunday afternoon, the storm is supposed to hit. Right on schedule, the wind picks up to a fresh breeze, it starts to rain, and then the first ice starts bouncing off the ground. For three days, Wally has repeatedly explained everything. "Folks, our wild west wind will bring in a pocket of low-lying cold air from inland, and when it meets the relatively warm ocean front laden with excessive moisture, that moisture will form into ice crystals by the time it hits the cold ground."

By dark, we're lights out and getting acquainted with the 1805 Beaufort Scale.

"Beaufort created a qualitative, objectively-based scale that mariners and lands-men alike could use to accurately describe and record wind conditions," my mother explains.

According to the Irish hydrographer Francis Beaufort, who would later become Rear Admiral Sir Francis Beaufort of the Royal Navy, we're sliding into Force 7, 35 MPH sustained wind, a near gale.

"Boys, if we were sailing with Great Great Great Great on the *Hurrying Angel*, we'd be seeing the waves heaping up with white foam. Now, look out the window. Whole trees are in motion."

We light the ancient kitchen candle chandelier that has been used as a decora-tion for my entire life, and watch the town below us go dark in sections.

"Don't worry boys, this old house was built to withstand the storms of Normandy. Indeed, she's a great ship on land. We should take a moment and thank Great, Great, Great, Great for his foresight, generosity, diligence, hard work, family-focus, not to mention considerable guile."

We all lower our heads in a mock period of silence.

Truth is, local historians refer to the man as an "opportunistic pirate and privateer who buried ill-gotten treasure in and around the shores of Kittery, Maine"; however, our mother holds a different opinion on the subject. Since the cradle, we've been told that her Great Great Great Great Grandfather, Captain Spencer Victor Wright, was a brave sea captain, an astute businessman who was gentle, kind-hearted, and altruistic. Great Great Great Great brought our entire manor house back from France during the Reign of Terror, stick by stick. On his last trip, he even brought over an extended family of French carpenters, the LaFramboises, to put the house together for him on top of Pulpit Bluff, that was three hundred feet above a protected deep water cove, with a stretch of fine sandy beach. Story goes that while the *Hurrying Angel* was away at sea, Great Great Great Great Grandmother Mahitable had acquired the bluff with a mile of coast line, cove, beach, a five acre barrier island that was a mile out to sea, fifty acres of woods, young orchard, and an extensive sheep pasture on top of the bluff in trade for a three bushel barrel of golden Normandy wheat. Supposedly, for years, Horace Kelsey, the deep pockets banker in Portsmouth, boasted to his big-pants cronies how he had bested Mahitable in business because her man was away at sea, and no one was there to do the thinking. I imagine the conversation went like this: "Hey, have some bread, boys, and I hope Mahitable enjoys herself rowing across the choppy Piscataqua at high tide on her way into town. Ha, Ha, Ha, Ha, Ha."

Our mother told us that Mahitable and Victor would sit in the firelight of this very same hearth and raise a glass of Port to Horace every Christmas eve with the toast, "What fools these mortals be."

For a number of years, Great Great Great Great had a good thing going with his ship, the *Hurrying Angel,* a former East Indiaman trader that no one really understands how he got his hands on. For a "reasonable fee" Victor smuggled out French aristocrats in hogshead wine barrels, along with an entire manor house, exquisite furnishings of one kind or another, and objects made of precious metals. In addition, he was interested in coin and jewels. He dropped off the aristos in Philadelphia, sailed up to Maine where he deposited the goods with Great Great

Great Great Grandma Mehitable; loaded up with lumber, fur, and fish; sailed back; sold that stuff to the Dutch, Portuguese, or Spanish—whoever would pay him the most; and then put his smuggling hat back on.

All goes well for six voyages, but coming back on the seventh, he gets pulled over by a French Corsair with forty cannon. When the French captain boards the *Hurrying Angel,* Victor explains that he's all-American—a neutral, not part of their war, and not up for grabs. The French captain snorts over his cologne, gets tough and says he and his boys don't always play by the rules. They now own everything, ship included. Great Great Great Great and his boys say I don't think so, overwhelm the boarding party and hold them hostage. With a musket barrel to the French captain's nose, Victor instructs the forty cannons to drift off or it's going to be hole in the head for Captain Cologne. The gentleman's agreement is that the captain and company will be set loose in their boarding boat at dark, and that they will not follow. Great Great Great Great keeps up his end of it, but when the Frenchies start drifting away, they all holler at the top of their lungs, trying to signal their ship that's lurking out there in the black soup.

The French captain supposedly vows revenge. He shouts, "Va cuisinar ton proper cul. Je te chie au cou." Translation: "Go cook your own arse. I shit down your neck."

Great Great Great Great, who spoke five languages according to our mother, sends a musket ball into the floor of the boat, right next to the Captain Cologne's feet. "Vous pouvez essayer tout ça, Huitre Bite, mais vous allez devoir sécher d'abord. Par coïncidence, je chie sur votre visage." Translation : "You can try all that, Oyster Dick, but you will have to dry out first. Coincidentally, I shit on your face."

Great Great Great Great lives to tell the tale, but when he arrives in Maine, Great Great Great Great Mehitable has other plans for the future, and the *Hurrying Angel* is sold to the Proprietors of the Portsmouth Pier, a colonial incorporation of entre-prenuerish merchants. However, Mehitable instructs the La Framboise family to remove the gold  lettered teak name board on the ship's bow and place it over the front entrance of our house. That's why, since 1798, our place has been called the Hurrying Angel.

My mother raises her face to the windows and eye-rolls when a gust smacks the house.

"You can shake and howl all night out there in your wolf suit, Mr. Wind, but these three little pigs aren't opening the door."

My mother sticks her tongue out when the next volley of freezing rain hits the windows like birdshot. Even my brother laughs.

In musical accompaniment with the wind, we all hear the growl and chain rattle of the sand truck coming up our hill, and then a strange glow appears in the tree canopy outside. Our entire ice-crystalled white oak woods rainbows to the revolving light of the truck. The rainbow light spreads to all of our faces, the white plaster walls of the house, the wide French parquetry oak and tile floor. It completely covers King Fergus, the long-haired six-toed bob-tailed tiger tom cat in my mother's lap. All of us, everything, lights up for the time it takes the sand truck to drive past our place. All of us sit open-mouthed, mesmerized, floating in the ocean of ice crystal refraction. All of us fall under the spell of the light.

"That guy must be having one hell of a night," I say. "We get to live inside a crystal chandelier for a short minute, but he gets it for an entire shift."

My brother coughs as he's sipping his hot chocolate, trying to stifle a laugh. He's way too old to laugh at a fifth grader's jokes. He lifts his eyes off the fire and looks at us both, and then lowers his sights on Mom. I don't like it. He has his pitcher's face on. He glances at the hardball he carries around in his left hand and adjusts his grip. I look at it, too. A while back, Jake had taken the time to show me all the grips of the pitches he throws. He is holding onto a four seam fastball.

"So how in the world did you even end up with *him*?"

The question circles in the air around us, lands on our shoulders, and then bites down hard on all the soft flesh around our necks. There's only one 'him' in our house, but for now that cat's away. We play.

When my mother laughs, though, the firelight on her face makes her look like she's eighteen. Her eyes gleam as she stares into the coals.

"OK, boys, I'll tell you if you're really interested."

She sits shoulders back and chin up in her uncomfortable chair, the side-effect of those years of ballet and tap lessons she had as a kid.

"Frank Holcolm was the first boy who took me on a date—well, sort of, I guess. Your grandfather drove us down to Peachy's Drug Store and Soda Fountain, sat in the car listening to the Red Sox without Ted Williams while Frank and I shared a banana split.

She throws her head back, laughs, and then narrows her eyes.

"The ice cream sure didn't last long around that boy. Splitting food of any kind was an 80/20 affair. Frank's father owned the hardware store and lumberyard in Portsmouth. He was a big tall man who looked like he was always receiving some bad news. Frank worked for him every day after school, sometimes in back of the counter, sometimes in the yard. Frank was getting groomed for a take-over, but he was pretty well-groomed to begin with. Lord have mercy, that boy loved money. Once he took me to the movies, and I watched him smile when he received his change. I watched him stroke a five dollar bill like it was a puppy's belly."

My brother's sipping his hot chocolate with his right hand, staring into the fire, but I know he's listening. He keeps on adjusting his grip on the hardball in his left. When his fingers find the curve, they stop. My mother glances back again at the long eighteenth century windows when the wind gives them a good shake.

"Frank joined the Marines immediately after graduation, fought at Guadalcanal, and was severely wounded. He said when the medics carried him out, he had to hold on to his stomach tight or his guts would fall out. When he came back, he asked me to marry him. I was doing homework in the old Portsmouth Academy Building Library, and he told me the only thing that kept him alive was the thought of me waiting for him back home. He said he held himself together knowing that I was on the other end.

My brother slowly turns and looks at her. For once, he's not playing baseball between his ears.

"I held his hand under the table. I told him I was sorry that I couldn't marry him. Why I didn't love him, I just don't know. He was big, handsome, and rich. One afternoon at the town pool, he dove off the high dive over thirty times trying to impress me. When I told him no, he started to tear-up, and I held his hand under the table. I held it hard and said I was sorry."

My brother sets his ball down, takes a bite off his enormous hot dog, chews it slowly, and then stares back at it like it's talking to him.

"How rich, Mom?"

My mother just looks at him and raises her eyebrows.

"Frank ended up marrying Sally Goodwin, one of my girlfriends and moved his business to Cape Cod. They had a pile of kids, and the last time I passed through Falmouth, they were living in the biggest house in town with an Olympic-size pool out back. Frank kept everything immaculately. When I drove by, he was washing his brand new metallic blue Oldsmobile convertible that was already spotless. I didn't stop, but I did notice, when he turned to see who was driving by, that he had a fallen face like someone had just delivered some bad news."

My brother cracks a big grin.

"Did that pool have a driving board?"

My mother nods and raises one eye brow.

"High dive."

The wind throws some more birdshot at the windows and the entire house sizzles. I'm thinking it might be gusting to full gale, force 8. There's got to be twenty foot waves out there and spindrift. My mother and brother start laughing when they see me ducking down in my chair, but our *Hurrying Angel* remains steadfast and holds her course.

"Both King Louis XVI and the Dauphin stayed in this house. According to Great Great Great Great, Louis would swing over to the coast of Normandy and meet his mistress under this roof."

My brother rumbles in laughter.

"Mom, are you telling us that Great Great Great Great bought a French whore house and brought it to America. Any chance we have any of that Dauphin in the wood pile?"

He pumps his eyebrows and tilts his head upward.

"I bet if we make a thorough search of the upstairs wardrobes, we'll find the long lost Dauphin hiding in his royal blue silk shorts."

My mother giggles, and the firelight performs its magic on her face.

She places both hands over her heart and then freezes with her theatrical-in-love-moony-Romeo's-soliloquy face on. She looks like Grace Kelly in Hitchcock's *To Catch a Thief*, looking up into the face of Cary Grant.

"Dauphin, Dauphin, 'O, that I were a glove upon that hand,

That I might touch that cheek!'"

Three seconds later she's shaking her head.

"Then there was Bill Wyatt. Bill was the strong silent type. He had a face like a Greek god's, gentle, mannerly. He was great at speaking with your grandfather. 'Oh yes, Mr. Wright. Oh no, Mr. Wright.' Bill was a master at asking my parents questions about their lives and work, but he had absolutely no sense of guile or irony: he was truly interested. I just have to say that I can't sit on the edge of my chair during the discussion of oil chemistry and middle management. 'Your father is a fascinating man,' Bill said once in all seriousness.

"Boys, let me tell you something. Your grandfather is a big-hearted man, he's a wealthy man, he's a generous man, he opens his checkbook with his heart, and he takes care of every leaf on his tree, we wouldn't be here without him, he gave us the *Hurrying Angel* to live in for the rest of our lives, but your grandfather is one of the most boring men the good lord ever put together—with the exception of Bill Wyatt. We'd go to a dance, and Bill would box step the entire night, when sometimes a girl has to Lindy Hop.

She throws her left leg up in the air, and Butch sits up, full moon-eyed.

"It got so that Bill would bore me even when he wasn't around. I just had to think about Bill and my shoulders would slump. It got so that when he showed up, I'd run and hide in an upstairs wardrobe with the Dauphin. Your grandmother had to deal with him. Good god, she got mad. Wouldn't give it up. 'JoAnn, you have one of the nicest, sweetest boys in the world, and you're going to lose him.'

" 'Moma, all of us are condemned to a death, but the worst kind of death is to be bored to death.' When she started to laugh, that was the end of Bill."

The beans have just begun to bubble, and the three chocolate browned Cornish game hens on the eighteenth century spit slowly spin around. During the early afternoon, my mother had rubbed a salt mixture into their skins that included parsley, sage, rosemary, and thyme. She had been singing the old folk tune, "Scarborough Faire" under her breath ever since. "Remember me to the one who lives there…" Already, I believed it was the fireplace. When we first got the thing going, she addressed it like she was Vanessa Redgrave onstage, pulling back, then pushing forward her hands, quoting Nathaniel Hawthorne this time in a clipped, haunting English accent.

"Where is that brilliant guest, that quick and subtle spirit, whom Prometheus lured from heaven to civilize mankind and cheer them in their wintry desolation; that comfortable inmate, whose smile, during eight months of the year, was our sufficient consolation for summer's lingering advance and early flight?"

Our mother explained that Hawthorne condemned the cast iron wood stove as an abomination to man's imagination. Nathaniel, according to our mother, suggested that when houses lost their fireplaces, they lost their doorways into other worlds, that for us included Louis XVI, the Dauphin, aristocrats stowed deep in the hull in hogshead barrels, 85 mph fastballs low and inside, and our own personal version of Dracula who was away for a blissful month on a business trip, sucking other people's blood on an entirely other continent.

Fergus is up again for a moment in my mother's lap, stretches out his huge front six-toed paws and begins kneading some cat bread on my mother's ancient teal green Merino wool shawl. She looks back into the coals, and Nathaniel's door opens a little wider.

"John Rasmussen was my beau when I was a senior in high school. We were inseparable, even though we were separated. He was there poolside when I won the state backstroke championship, and he was poolside when I lost my chance to go to the Olympics by a whisker. John put his arms around me, and that's all I needed. That boy was a healer. He could take a crying, colicky baby and make him jump for joy. He took me to the senior prom, and he'd hitchhike home every other weekend from the University of Minnesota where he was going to med school. 1,500 miles. Weather never discouraged him. He hitch-hiked home in a blizzard once, and got a ride from the state police, which he could never stop talking about. He was twenty-one, and if he could get his hands on his grandfather's model A, we'd drive around town and act like gangsters. John had the most incredible James Cagney impression.

She leans forward, screws up her face, and points at the fire like her hand is a gun. Butch jumps off her lap.

"'Call me Rassy, see, that is if you don't want to become a bucket that can't hold water. Hey! Anybody here want to get introduced to my heater?'

"He'd stuff his right hand into the front pocket of his overcoat and act like it was a pistol. Whenever John came back from school, he was one wild boy, should have been chained up to a tree somewhere. Once after his finals, he hitchhiked all night to see me, tapped on my window at 3:30 in the morning, and kissed me through the screen."

Fergus wanders back and is just about to jump back on her lap when her Cagney voice scares him off again.

"'Look here, Peaches. I'll be back at 6:00 this evening. We'll get two Delmonicos and seats at the Roxy.' That was John talk for a dinner and a movie."

The wind blows a good moaning gust against our ancient diamond windows. In the circle of light from our house, I can see that the wind is breaking twigs off the trees and covering our yard in fine debris. From our qualitative observations, we're guessing that Iceageddon is pelting the coast with gusts up to force 9—that's 50 MPH on the Beaufort Scale—severe gale. The sea begins to roll.

"Mom, it sounds like there's an old man out there throwing handfuls of gravel at the house."

Jake stands up and points.

"There he is in his big black hat."

My brother explodes in laughter when I jump up and look out the window. My mother goes on, framed in the fireplace light.

"John's father was a wealthy lawyer, but was the kind of person who would never think of giving his son any money. And John, for his part certainly wasn't afraid of work. He worked construction every summer and pick up jobs whenever he could, but that spring when he hitchhiked home, I learned later that he had seventeen cents in his pocket."

My brother takes a bite of his foot long dog and speaks while he is chewing a mouthful.

"So John was going to buy you a candy bar for dinner?"

My mother makes her absolute affirmation face. She curls her lips inward, and then gently bites down, nodding her head.

"Absolutely nothing could hold that boy back. After stopping by to see me, he went out on the highway and knocked over Benny's."

"Benny's?"

My brother cocks his head to the side, the way I had seen hunting dogs do when they get off the scent.

As she speaks, my mother's smile spreads across her face, deep nod.

"Benny's was an all-night truck stop out on Route 1 where, according to Johnny, if you ate there, you'd get free gas all night. He walked up right after seeing me, slipped a nylon stocking over his head with his slouchy Hamburg hat and knocked over Benny's."

"What's that mean?" I ask.

My brother looks at me like he is the owner of the bird dog that lost the scent.

"Her boyfriend robbed the place."

My mother sips her hot chocolate, and tightens her face, and gives us her version of Cagney.

"'Now, see here Benny, give me every fin and sawbuck in that cash ringer or you'll be using your face to drain spaghetti.' Unbeknownst to me, John got away with forty-five dollars. We went out to the Piscataqua Steak House for the

Delmonicos, and then we saw *Double Indemnity*, armed with a pad and paper. For months afterwards, John could slip into Fred MacMurray at a moment's notice, said I was far better looking than Barbara Stanwick. 'I'm crazy about you, Baby' called me 'doll face'. John could never get over the plot, though. Every once in a while he'd turn to me and say, 'I know, we'll murder your husband, make it look like he fell off a train by accident, collect double on the secret life insurance policy we took out on him, and live happily ever after. Nobody will ever figure it out. Sound good?'

"After the movie that night, we actually drove to Benny's. John had a beer while I had a black raspberry ice cream cone. He withheld the robbery information from me for about a year."

"How was Benny taking it?" my brother asks.

My mother opens her hands and offered them to the fire, palms down.

"Benny told us that he had been robbed by ten men, all toting Thompson sub-machine guns. The next day, there was an anonymous donation of 39 dollars to the Portsmouth hospital. During his confession to me about a year later, John explained that it was for all those people who ate at Benny's and had to go to the emergency room afterwards. 'As long as the emergency room has plenty of Milk of Magnesia, plenty of open windows, and nobody lights a match, this place can go forth and thrive; otherwise, the whole town's going to blow.'

"When John graduated from med school, he appeared at my window in the 3:00 A.M. moon shine. He had a white gardenia in his lapel that was just a couple of shades lighter than his towhead hair. Of course, he was wearing his black slouch hat. We're there on different sides of the screen, it's May, peepers in full voice. He's all Cagney. 'Let's scram up to Minnesota, Doll Face.' He had landed an internship at the Mayo Clinic's Eugenio Litta Children's Hospital. His dream job. And then, on the other side of the screen, he reaches into his pocket, says, 'Look, see, I got a heater in my pocket that's going to open the safe,' but he pulls out a small black box, opens it, and there's his great grandmother's diamond ring."

My brother shakes his head in the firelight.

"You don't have to tell us what happened next, but you do have to tell us what happened to John."

"By thirty-five, my gangster boy became the chief heart surgeon at the Mayo Clinic. He particularly loved working with children."

We all listen to the birdshot and moan of the freezing rain and wind for a while. The whirl of the eighteenth century state-of-the-art rotisserie spinning our Cornish game hens sounds a little like the fluttering of small birds. Nathaniel was right: why would anyone want a cast iron wood stove that makes a prisoner of your fire when you could stare right into the flames and see the past and the future unfold at your warm feet. I stare at the flames and start to think that maybe my mother's story is a lot like Sherry Thompson's that I had heard the year before in fourth grade. For her tenth birthday present, her grandfather gives her the pick of litter of his eight Golden Retriever puppies. Sherry, with the tenderness and wisdom of her new double digits, chooses the monster. Her pup viciously bites her, every member of her immediate family, the baby sitter, and the mailman. That dog goes on to chew huge holes in every one of her mother's priceless heirloom oriental rugs, topping things off by killing the neighbor's fourteen year-old cat. One day when Sherry returns from school, she's told that her father has taken Daisy to live on a farm in New Hampshire, where she can live out the rest of her life without hurting anyone or anything else.

I mention Sherry's story again to my mother and brother.

My brother spins the hard ball in his hand, and gives me his strike three face. I check his grip: slider. He speaks to our mother.

"Must be a farm across the river in New Hampshire somewhere that would take that bastard. That 'Live free or die' crowd has no standards.

From now on, I'm calling that bastard 'Pick-of-the-litter."

Our mother highly approves of the name and takes a moment to explain something about verbal irony that I really don't get.

"That's right," I say. "He's a baby-puke yellow pick-of-the-litter bastard."

Our laughter is in full concert with the gale. Regardless, our mother manages to give us both another curt nod.  Yes, indeed: Montevideo is the capital of Uruguay.

Four weeks later my father returned from his European business trip and spent the first day railing about the junk lamps we had forgotten to return to the attic. He railed about how stupid we all were to waste all that wood during the power outage, and how everything in the house smelled like smoke. He really exploded when he discovered that one of his uncomfortable Bergman chairs had a small circle of melted plastic in the seat, probably from a thrown spark from the fireplace. The morning after his return, my mother showed up at breakfast, tight lipped with small purple bruises on her neck and arms.

But for now, we are all on this side of the dirt and hearthside. Great Great Great Great's *Hurrying Angel* holds fast, resolute in the fresh gale, and the old man throwing gravel at the house is getting nowhere. The green red wood tree on my brother's crimson Stanford sweatshirt is absorbing another barrage of ketchup from his second foot-long dog, King Fergus is kneading another loaf of cat bread on my mother's lap, and I'm wearing my coonskin cap and sheath knife. I take a moment and set up two more chairs in our semi-circle of light. Both my mother and brother lift their hands, looking for an explanation.

"Well, one's for King Louis XVI, and the other one's for the Dauphin. I don't want either of them to think that we're the kind of people who hold back on a dry spot by the fire and a full plate of beans, game hen, and greens."

All of us turn to the windows when we hear the rumble, rattle, and clank. The sand truck is making its way up our hill at a good four miles an hour again. We all watch it throw its beam through our canopy of white oaks. The ice-encased trees, the ice-covered ground, our diamond windows, plaster walls, wide board Frenchy floors—all of it could have been on fire, every surface prismatic.

I hold my breath and bite down hard. I see it again. My mother and brother are smiling. We are all smiling in the rainbow light.

**Celebrating Gary Snyder's Birthday–**
**May 8ᵗʰ at the Emily Proctor Shelter**
**–Vermont Long Trail**

After three days of hard rain, the sun
rises clear and strong, and the news
falls out of the public radio for each
creature and blade of grass, so I
too the trumpet in respectful
tellurian response

                 –my way, that is, which  means
forget work and take off with my outlaw
logger boots, rucksack, driving to the trail
head in deep conversation singing: Hello
Great Beings without number

                    –and soon
Mother Earth is pushing my vibram soles
along the Great Moose Highway, or the Great
Moose Rest Stop with the New Haven River too
spring fat to ford, so I mad dash

                     up-stream, jumping
boulder
      wild man–like you
              I mean, what's
the worry? You can't fall off a river. Isn't that
right? So I say: Courage
Brothers–in general to my

             considerable
vibrating audience–and glide
up-trail to the snow-line

                        —still up to your
hips, Creator. What's going on? Gasp
last mile.
            Step, sink
                    snow in your
belly-button, wet to the crotch, thinking
forget it, world gone grey, freezing, red
hands, old man, bad knees
                        —Great Protectors, global
failure, hatred, regret, turn around, endless
sorrow
        tumbling in the Samsara
Machine, and one hundred steps later, I
arrive at the white sun-boned shelter
–wringing out my socks, boots on warm
boards
        —clean red toes clinging to the spine
of heaven.

## Projecting a Major Exchange
## on the Train with Mr. Olsen

The seven triangular pieces of wood he wildly
strapped to an ancient traditional pack transformed
themselves into the boat he used to fish the mountain
lake, and he lived in a cave up there, slept
on pine boughs, had a wolf and a reindeer
for pets. He drew us pictures of them like his
hands were enchanted–a wolf and a reindeer
smiling, a wolf and a reindeer who
loved each other like husband and wife. His

wife had died years before while he was clerking
at the bank. He must have been counting
money, he said, and when he came home his
house was empty except for his life-long
collection of clocks and their incessant
ticking.
      He nodded and turned to the conductor who
was his best friend, or maybe the conductor
was his brother–regardless, these two old men could
stand in each other's company not saying
a word, smiling and nodding in their
ridiculous silent reverie, forever
chewing on mouthfuls of nothing. When the train

slowed to a crawl in the middle of nowhere, they
off-loaded his supplies, but when it came
time for him to grab his pack and go, I

might have grabbed it instead and jumped. I
might have jumped a few seconds before the train
regained speed–and there would not have been one
word of protest, only kind-hearted
waves from the old man and the conductor, even
the engineer. You see, this is how it might

have happened–the two day hike to the green
mountain lake–a wolf and a reindeer running
to greet me, the smell of pine boughs as I
fell asleep in the cave, firelight
reflecting off the stone ceiling.
     And this is how
I might have come to fall through the ice one
spring as I shuffled back home from a ski–wet
worn-out, and then the world going
light to dark–cold, numb, and then
nothing–
  or maybe I might have just triumphantly
met the train every year, the engineer
blowing the whistle, the conductor shouting
thick hoarse laughter, the incredulous round
faces of passengers in the windows, as if
I had grown antlers and hooves. And this is how I

might have even taken the rarefied, unparallelled
opportunity to extend my quiet compassionate
hand warmly to young travelers, proclaiming
–with the grin of a moose– that Oh, yes. I'm extraordinarily
glad to meet you, and by the way, I'm Lars Olsen

# Trying to Imagine Norman

Norman was the state high jump
champ who cleared 6'1" no
problem. Everybody comfortably
said he would be
something but Norman said he
imagined he already
was and laughed. He also laughed
a lot–had the dumbest laugh for such
a smart guy. Imagine
a human hyena. That

was Norm. Now, imagine
a human hyena with
a rifle. That was Norman
in Vietnam–shot an old
lady in half–watched red rice
push out the bullet holes while
humming a Beatles tune (Maxwell's
Silver Hammer.) "It helps to
abstract oneself," said Norm who
came of of the whole thing

without a scratch, except
the ones he put in his own
arm, which is to say Norm got
funny at home trying to feel
good. Tackled me on the street
when a truck backfired, Norm

screamed, "Incoming! Stay
down, Jimmy." And oh God, pissed
his pants in front of a whole
curious crew, so we had to get
drunk and/or stoned which is to say
Norm managed to stay smooth
until he fell into the spinach
at the A&P and never got
out because too much
smack. And of course he
drank as well. Still haunts
the vegetable aisle. Imagine
his howly voice back with fresh
giggles from way out there.

# underground

noun

ˈən-dər-ˌgraund : a subterranean space or channel

"The cave you fear to enter holds the treasure you seek."
—Joseph Campbell

"You have to get to where you can see the dark things in the dark box and ignore them. Not forget them. Not hide them. But you live side by side with them, you look them straight in the eye, and you no longer freak out. Then you are OK."
—Carl Jung

## Leonard Falls into the Impatiens

Days of reckoning. Days of Pain. It's the same
sad story. There were twenty-three champion
horses, living and dead, on a farm of cats
and dogs, the high lonesome sound of paint
peeling off the barn, a '68 Chrysler
Imperial, and a thousand blackbirds
roosting in three maple trees. And there was a nice
old man who built everything with a hammer. He was so
nice that even when he yelled, the horses stood
easy, the cats drank milk, and the dogs laughed. The birds
just sat in the trees. The sky was cobalt
blue, and at night the moon hung
low over the barn. Remember? This is the same

sad story you've always heard–the one where
an old man wakes up in the cobalt
blue night, makes his slow painful way down
steep stairs, pulls on his matching red plaid
coat and hat, bumbles out the kitchen
door only to fall face down in the flower bed. Sweet
earth, he thinks–because some has pushed up
into his mouth and nose. Sweet earth. He tries
to say this to himself before he dies. See? The horses

hang their heads, the birds fly out of the trees, the sky
turns black, and the dogs cry until they're
blind. Click bang goes everything shifting
to a new world order. Click bang. And this

is how I find him early the next morning–
because this is my story, too. I find him curled
up tight in the flower bed. So I
shake him. Nothing. So I shake him
again and shout: You're not dead! You're
never going to die!—and then one brown eye opens, a cough
full of dirt, and I say: It's all right. You've
done nothing wrong. No one's thinking you look
ridiculous with bent glasses and dirt
on your lips. In fact, you look good. And when I
pull him to his feet I say: You're looking

good. And it was true. He looked good in his
red plaid hat framed in cobalt blue, a thousand
blackbirds circling the maple trees, the jubilant
sound of horses raising their heads under
the moon in audible click bang, the dogs shouting, I
can see! I can see!—and a wide expansive smile
spreading across the chrome grill of the  Chrysler
Imperial, because this isn't the sad story you know
after all. There isn't even a day of reckoning, or a day
of pain. It's just the story of a nice

old man who sprouts wings out of his red
plaid jacket and flies away, and me standing
in front of a long, smooth dent in the impatiens
wondering if I've seen such a terrible
bright moon, or wondering if one of these days
we might be fortunate enough to get a little rain.

## Chenrezig Appears
## (At the Plainfield Thursday
## Evening Farmers' Market)

He was a big man, 6'2" or so, and he had a set of arms on him where the veins stuck out like a road map.  He walked upright, head high, but when he moved, he favored his right leg, and he had one of those grape juice birthmarks on his cheek, thick ice cream white wavy hair, and you couldn't help but notice that his jaw and teeth were too big for the rest of his face when he smiled, something kids would have ridden him about when he was in high school, but if I had to guess, I'd guess that for him high school was sixty years ago. He wore a filthy green John Deere hat, but his jeans were clean, out at the knees, but clean, and his black watch plaid shirt was out at the elbows.

Why I had an extra folding chair, I have no idea, but I instantaneously regretted it when he asked if he could sit a while. All day, everything had been breaking, myself included. Maybe it was the July 3 heat, but I was worn out with trying. I was done, out of ideas,  and I sat there surly and broken, but when we shook hands, something  shifted, and I couldn't help but smile.

The man had an intense grip, sure, but there was something wrong with his pinky. It dangled away from the other fingers. He saw me notice.

"That's what seventy years of milking looks like. You wouldn't believe that's what milking cows does to a hand, but it does."

He held up his left for me to see.

"Got another one just like it."

He received no argument from me. The hands were a perfect match.

"Hey, I got a thermos of iced coffee," I said. "You in the business?"

"Hell, yes. I'm not a man who passes up iced coffee on a scorcher like today. I'm glad somebody's doing the thinking."

He sat, and I poured some into a pint jar.

"Appreciate it. Oh good. It's black. There are places milk should not go and coffee's one of them. Don't care what the majority thinks. The majority voted for Richard Nixon in 1972. McGovern was ten times the man Nixon was, but Tricky won in a landslide."

He took a long sip. Big flash of white teeth.

"Good deal. No sugar. Stuff will kill you. Thank you. Just the way I like it. How did you know I was coming?"

He let out a laugh. We sat and sipped out of our jars, and we stared across the green of the Plainfield United Methodist Church at his rusty white rattle-trap Ford pick-up that was just about spilling over the wooden side rails with sweet corn. I couldn't imagine what he was thinking–that he actually thought he was going to sell all that. In this heat, it was going to be compost tomorrow. He nodded his head like I had just said something, and he was agreeing.

"Yes, Sir. I lost my wife Tuesday, July 1. I lost her to cancer. We fought it off for a while, but that son-of-a-bitch came back and got us. We were both nineteen when we got married. Fifty-seven years. I was in love the whole time, but she made it easy."

I was still in my thirties, and I didn't know what to say when someone hurt like that.

"You going to be alright?"

"Good god, that girl could dance. You'd swear she was full of feathers. We had kitchen hops back then. We'd sit the fiddler on top of a cold cook stove,  dance all night, and in the morning do chores. Am I going to be all right? Oh, yeah. I have a daughter and a son-in-law, and we've always been a close family. And can you believe I'm a grandfather?"

I opened my eyes wide and leaned forward a bit, shook my head, but honestly, I could believe he was a great-grandfather.

His voice caught on the edge of something, and I thought here it comes. Now he's going to fill a bucket. Instead, he nodded towards a man about my age, and a young woman unloading his truck, setting up an old door on saw horses, stretching out a red checkered oilcloth on top of it all. And there was a bunch of screaming kids jumping all over, two boys and a little girl, all three of them redheads.

"Sure, I'm going to be alright. It's just that I'm never going to see her again. That's the worse part. I'm OK with dying. Hell, I'm a farmer. The entire enterprise is about loss. We might as well be in the dying business. But I don't believe in a life hereafter. I don't believe that when I die, she'll be waiting for me on a white cloud playing a harp. I'm not churchy at all, but I do appreciate the United Methodists letting us use their parking lot. Nice people."

He took a sip of his coffee.

"That girl always knew what to do and what to say. The sky would start falling–no joke–and she'd be out there putting back the pieces. We had a hell hole of a little house when we were first married. She had made me this beautiful stuffed pork chop dinner, gravy, green beans, candle light. Rain storm came up, and it was leaking everywhere. Couldn't believe it. Water coming down everywhere, right on the table. It didn't even take the smile off her face. She opened an umbrella, sat on my lap, moved the plates and candle in close. After every bite, I'd give her a kiss. I did. The wood cook stove hissing away in back of us. Thunder rumbling. Apple pie à la mode. Just to look at her would take my breath away. That's who I'm never going to see again."

We went on to talk about loose-eyed and close-eyed sheep dogs, buckwheat rotation, haying and late July rain—until he let out a breath, stood up, shook my hand again.

"I started working for my dad when I was five, he paid me a dime a week, and even back then I thought it was fun. My father knew how to make it fun. We had a ball mostly. Farming's an affliction, a disease, and I see you have it."

The rest of the evening looked like he was conducting the Queen's Birthday Parade over at his table, the tiny red-haired girl riding horse on his shoulders, two little wild red wolf boys rolling in the dirt. By the time the lights went out, I had done OK, but he had sold everything, down to nothing. I saw him give away the last ear to a young woman pushing a stroller.

They rattle-trapped away, laughing, the son-in-law and daughter, little red bouncing on his lap, two Massai warriors riding in the back pounding on top of the cab, howling out "In the jungle the mighty jungle the lion sleeps tonight."

He pointed at me, waved, and then shouted something I didn't quite get. Still, I waved back, tried to say something, but ended up giving him back his own grin. I felt it in my face and hands, in my arms and shoulders. It wasn't the words I needed, anyway. That grin was all teeth and jaw.

# How I've Managed to Arrive So Late

Last night I woke up again in the lost dream
heat lightning Pennsylvania night with the fan
playing rolly polly circus music, rising
full orange Gypsy moon
                              gracious ground
swelling in syncopated rhythm and blues, Ira
Gershwin lyrics radiating over fields so
old, they have names
                          and several hundred
years of broken hearts to ensure endless
fertility
             so I got an insomniac bad
case of the goes and the get theres all
over again
                all at the same time, pulled my
hands off my intrepid ears
                              listened to my heart
beat and the all night mockingbird until

the years rose out of dark water–years
of leaving town in a broken rust bucket black
Ford, swimming in beers, wrong turns, laughs, big
presidential bills falling out of the holes
in my pockets
               –years of regroup, re-roof, resolve
running wild with the pretty roan horses, running
wild on hard feet, soft backs, and fat souls

–years of drunk off the road, belly-button
deep in the snow, over-throwing, over-
looking, overturning
                         –years of waiting for the cows
to come home
                  coming out vegetarian, getting
religion
         endless compassion, doing
some rather incredibly instinctive and imaginary
automotive paint and body work
                                    –years of speaking
in my patent, incomprehensible, you-got-to-
know-me-for-years-first, back
sliding stutter fashion
                          –years of barking
backwards during
                      metaphorical dog shows
–years of getting over-dogged, dogged down, dog
sat, dog-goned
                   –years of skinny dipping in all ice
cold mountain rivers without end
                                     –years of strange
and unlikely disappearances, shouting jumping-
Jehovah-out-the-window wolf calls, making
friends
         blood brother friends, inseparable, tele-
connected past-lifed strong-hearted tribal
warrior friends
                   –years of losing some friends
–years of walking all day and night, feet

on fire mountains, legs, heart, hair all
still in a blur
                    —years of moaning in love, I mean all
night deep-down, hands in my pockets, head
thrown back, pleading
                         face in the cosmos, listening
to the howling full wind moaning in love
                                    —years of falling
in general, of falling
                    through the ice, falling
off a few ladders and roofs, from relatively well
respected positions in the community
                              —years of
listening to the night vibrate up
                              the smoky rough
cut boards of my house, up the table legs, blue
bed stead, fine brick chimney
                         right through
the leaky roof and into the wandering sky
                                    —years
of honey brown beer, whiskey fiddle, staggering
across the stage
                    driving wildman
worn-out, empty, truck rattling, sloppy
hot, drifting all over the road
                         —years of silver
plane rides, mouthing idioms, roaches moon walking
out of the typewriter, hundred of young
people in cold classrooms with their
hearts in their gloved hands: poor boy, fat

girl, class clown with the flutter heart, sportsman
with the Parkinson shakes
                                    all needing
a brother, a father, all needing
                                         someone who would
walk with them to the end of the day
                                         —years of
waking up with a start in the middle of the coal
black night, stars, moons rising through
the window, and me sitting in perpetual
amazement, thinking if I listen
                                    if only I could
live with the dolphins, if only I could speak
dolphinese
              feel the tides rise and fall in my
blood
        —years of running the high mountain
back roads, my feet
                            landing in circles of antediluvian
dust, as I talk to the trail, as the trail
speaks back
                as the years compress themselves
like some fine crow got loose and laid
a track on my puppy belly face for every
time I've had a good laugh, which is to say, just

look at me. Can't you hear me laugh? Can you
recognize me? Can I even recognize
myself? Why, I was once
                            a boy in a coon skin cap

–and maybe I imagine all these years
someone's been waiting at a window, tapping
their foot, mildly annoyed, dinner on low, a pile
of dogs thumping their plumed and unwieldy
tails, poised for the heroic
sight of me.
        They know my voice will be
like a trumpet, my
chest like a bear's.
          Dressed in last year's bird
nests and dried herring, I will hold forth: my true
and unusual heart-felt explanation. Oh yes, my dear
friends, this is how I've managed to arrive so late.

# Who I Am and What I Want to Know

I'm the big howling laugh coming out of some fat
man's mouth, or the no-good work-a-holic Afro-
Jew lover man in the cold night–head down, hands
deep in the pockets of his ratcatcher jacket
–walking through the red brick town like he's got
somewhere to go.
                Or I'm the Yankee white boy, or the cold
disconcerted Saint horse's ass, or a barefoot Big Uncle Dim
Uncle (Yes, I'm staying for lunch, Little Honey) Uncle
Captain my Captain Baby James–the sailor man–hard
to hold Darling-Boy, cruising Shanghai (Oh–the troubles
I've seen) Jack Black Dog–Attorney at Law, Long
Gone Dean, Strong Heart Running Coyote Man is who I


am. And what I want to know Father Judas Priest, Brother
Bone Face, Sister Mary Jumping Jehovah Holy Roaming
Angel Girl, Mister–Look, I forget your name–but can you
tell me please–if you could make her alive again
would she still know my face after all these years?

**"Once a Jolly Swagman"**
A Peripheral Account of Significant and Verifiable Details
(That Must Be Remembered As the Family Moves Forward)

He loved the military but fainted at the sight of blood. He was
tone deaf and often sang "Santa Lucia."  Over the course of his
lifetime, he attended the changing of the guard thirty-
seven times.

        He started falling out of bed. It sounded like
snow sliding off the slate roof. We brought in an electrified
hospital model with security rails to fence him in.


He used the expression "Not a leaf on my tree."  He
used the expression, "She's a good egg."


Once, when I offered ice cream, he thought I said
"Raspberry Squirrel." His voice could carry across three
football fields. He created a Christmas tree farm. He called
Christmas trees "boys."
        As an undergraduate, he was hot ironed
branded on the soft tissue of his left pectoral with the Greek letters Delta Kappa
Epsilon.
        He would have honorably sailed with
Viscount, 1st Duke of Bronte, Vice-Admiral of the White, Lord
Horatio Nelson.
        A substitute home health aide showed up
with a crackling hack cough. "Nothing stops me," she said. "I have
animals. I have eleven bee hives."
        "Are bees animals?" I asked.
She hacked back with her red face, "Well, they're not plants."

He was almost 96.

After he fell out of bed, he pulled the blankets over his shoulders
and fell asleep on the floor until help arrived.
                                    He carried
a genetic predisposition to distrust the French. He cried
at the death of the ancient little black farm dog who slept at his
feet.
        He called out from the dark room, "Got any of that ice cold
orange juice?" He was tone deaf and sang "Waltzing Matilda."

His favorite movie was *Gunga Din.*

He played right guard on the Middlebury College
football team. His number was 29. In four years, he
competed on the gridiron for about a minute and a half.

He'd catch red squirrels under his lake camp with
a Have-A-Heart trap. Afterwards, he'd walk to the end
of the dock, throw the trap in the water, and read *The New York Times.*

He died in my wife's arms.

He scrounged old timbers, toilets, and doors, and built five
houses over the course of his lifetime. They all had academy
award-winning  southern exposure with Greyhound bus bathrooms.

He kept a cache of used Kleenex in the basket of his walker.

He taught economics, history, and math at a prep school
in New Hampshire. He threw erasers in class. Once, he threw
a bucket of water on a sleeping quarterback.  Once, he
made a bad boy sit in the trash can.

When he

awoke in the morning, he said, "Hitler must have been
crazy to think that he could take over the world." When he
awoke in the morning, he said, "I'm sorry I made
a mess." When he awoke in the morning, he said, "Don't
leave me. I'm dying."


He was the fastest man on the Kimball Union Academy hockey team.
His favorite book was *The Merry Adventures of Robin Hood*.


He called out from the dark room, "Hey. There's
a guy in here trying to sleep."


He kept faith and held supreme confidence in the New York Giants.


Everyone was up all night. Fluid filled his chest. His cough
sounded like a rifle report. We called
for oxygen. We went through an entire jumbo package
of disposable underwear. When I ran for
back-up, the young pharmacist told me that I'd find
the store brand far superior: "Great fit. Supreme
comfort. You'll like them. No leakage."


He reroofed an entire lake camp solo when he was 86.

He wrote seven grandchildren generous checks the week before he died.
He went 1 and 9 his first season as Varsity Football Coach. At the suggestion
that he drop down to JV, he said:

"My furniture has wheels."


His hair was still red well into his 80s.
He called my wife "The 8th Armored Division."


The Hospice nurse said, "Maybe today." Then she shrugged her
shoulders and tilted her head. "Tonight?"


He said, "Don't worry. Trump will never last." He said, "The Japanese
must have been crazy to think they could beat us. Yamamoto
had toured Detroit. He saw what we could do."


The Hospice nurse said she also had chickens that laid blue eggs.


He said I wore my hat like the garbage men from White Plains, NY.


He donated his body to science. He returned two years later impersonating
grey dust in a quart jar.

My wife said that during their
family cross-country road trip, a monster torrential thunderstorm
came up out of nowhere at the campground. She said he
ran around with the stew pot on his head and made everybody laugh.


When he awoke, he said he had been talking with his grandmother.


"Really?" I said. "How is she?"

He shook his head side to side on the pillow.

"Funny. She's so funny. We were snapping green beans on her back
porch with the sky blue ceiling. Yes. We were. She said 'Spencer,
there's so much to do here. I could really could use your help with the lambs this spring.'
I told her I was on my way."

## "Oh, The Places You Can Go"

"Congratulations!
Today is your day. You're off to Great Places! You're off and
away!"

—Seuss


Roll in her arms—you lose your body.


Roll in her arms—you lose everything
all the chips and cards

        the sum of what
you have been

      who you are, everything
to be will shed its skin in photographic
flash and form.


    Wrapped up
tight in her arms, you can become
a runner tumbling through astronomical
night. Why, you can watch your delirious
feet catch fire.


    —That's right—
for you oblivion can have a smile on its face
or the road can rise

       invisibly at the speed
of sound and light.

     —Yeah, Boy—miles
in ten directions can wave

you and your sorry dog ears home

or miles can call the rhythm
of your breathing outward
                    into a foggy
river
        into a sea of falling stars.

# Coasting Down Taylor Avenue
## On Bob's Birthday

Most of the action had already taken place in Bob's well-organized garage/work-
shop,  but there were still
a significant number of excellent
choices.
>There was drunk
and soda; a myriad of vanquished, gold-edged
plates with toothpicks, and most of a famous
pork-rice dish brought by Bob's Chinese friend
Chen. On the workbench by the band saw stood
a pyramid of feather-lite egg white
cookies, evidently Bob's favorite—who was a little
heavy, wore sandals, cargo shorts, a purple
t-shirt, and didn't say much except, "Thanks," but no one
could blame him. He was an engineer who had somehow
made it to fifty, and he even rode with a pack
of bi-polar, high-fiving Ninja motorcyclists.

After the cake and toast, Bob's boys seriously
revved ensemble, spun a few
doughnuts in the yard to delight the children—and then
roared off into the towering, fresh-cut grass
Rockwellian, mid-summer darkness
>>—at which time
Bob's sister commented that he, Bob, could
spell his name frontwards or backwards with absolutely
no lexicological derivation. She went on to say
that at death, John Wayne's colon weighed

eighty pounds. The Duke was certainly a big
man, someone said; still, I'm sure all of us
silently hoped we'd tip the scales at considerably
less when our time came.
                                 After the invitation to join
your women friends, the children, and Bob's
Plott coon dog, Chief, for campfire s'mores, I shook
Bob's hand and told him. "You're doing everything
right," although I had no idea. Regardless, Bob seemed
to agree, and fifteen minutes later, you and I
peddled off, floating up Devino Street to Mountain, past
the Stephen Newton Elementary School, all the way to Taylor
Avenue, where we took a right down the unusually
steep hill.
                    I reached out through the night and touched
your arm, just for a second, and then coasted
up into the black maple canopy, past
all the yellow porch lights and golden retrievers
asleep on rag-rug welcome mats, rising faster past
the bark and leaves into the blue-black, no
stars, no steeple, speeding past
the idea of all the white lead clapboard
towns and broken hill farms, old chubby near-sighted
women with calico cats on their wide laps, yellow
roses along a busted cedar fence line rising
off the edge of the map into no air, no
face, all eyes, and nothing to see for black hole miles.

When we pulled up even at the stop sign on North, I
kissed you deep on the lips and said, "Now, Darling, I'm

sticking with you like raspberry jam on toast, until
all the lights go out, until dogs don't have
tails, until you hear music every time you see my big
bad road face."
    And you kissed me back, long and slow, not
knowing that I had just died a little
          which makes these days
just more connected tales out of the Book
of Revelations, I guess—the dirty dishes, twisted
egg encrusted spoons and forks, the skunk inspired
in-town compost pile, week-old *Sunday Times,* clementine
peels, kids' clothes covering the heirloom, oriental
dog hair floor. I could put my face into my
indelibly dirty hands and howl in ten
directions, which is to say, I'm
coasting, Brother Bob, anyway
you spell it, congratulations. Happy
birthday. It's a miracle.

# The Way It Is Deep in the Frozen Lake

Months later she had gotten
use to the cold, and the way
her long, chestnut
hair swirled around her face. Her
mouth was frozen as if, with exquisite
elocution, she died pronouncing the word
"So."
     He died with a half-way
grin thinking something was actually
funny—maybe the way the ice
roared when it broke, or the way
the lights stayed on for nearly
a minute. Or maybe he grinned because
he drove across the lake in the first
place thinking it was
a short-cut, because he wanted
to buy some beer. And how
absurd. There was no
beer down there. So, you see. This
accounts for the grin.
          And his
hands had come off the door latch, floated
under the wheel, and every
few weeks he touched her almost
apologetically—and then floated
back. And every few weeks her hands
hunted his, as her hair swirled
out of her beautiful

purple face, she would
stare at him. She would
stare at him for weeks, her
mouth curled delicately
—as if she were saying the word, "So."

# Champ, The Movie Dog, Speaks

Fresh out of the army, I could only land bit parts: the Dalmatian in the firehouse
funeral parade, the lost Jack Russell pup looking for his
master on a corpse-strewn Normandy beach. I jumped through a couple of windows for Lassie, fought off wild boars for Old Yeller, took a bullet for the Biscuit
Eater. I was even the voice of Bugle Anne.

But soon I was doing side-kick roles: Clark Gable's hound dog, Bill
Bailey, in *The Misfits*. I was Sam, growling at Apaches with the Duke in *Hondo*, and
then before I knew it, I was Rin Tin Tin; Benji; Toto; Nikki—Dog of the North;
Sandy, Fly, the Tramp, Big Red; Sounder.

I was leading cavalry charges, getting tossed out of white
water canoes, killing cougars. I played both canine leads in *The Incredible Journey*.
I played Buck, lap dog turned brute,  in *The Call of the Wild.*

And as you sat, a little kid in the theater, thick scratchy wool seat poking through
your sear sucker shorts, I was the dog who grabbed your hand and led you through
the burning farmhouse, the dog who lay over you while you slept, lost on Mad Wolf
Mountain, twenty below, the storm of the century raging all around you. I was the
dog who pulled you through six miles of North Atlantic chop when your fishing
boat went down, the dog who bit the grin right off the face of your evil, drunken
step-father.

And when I died on screen, you were nothing but a bucket of tears, sitting in the
darkness,  pitching in a rough salty ocean of grief—and then spilling out into the
post-cinematic air still teary from the twenty-one gun salutes of farewell, graveside canine  prayers, the rain coming down hard as the baleful cinematic family,
all adorned in exquisite 1890 Victorian mourning attire, places a stone a-top my

freshly turned grave. Outside the theater, your mother pulled you into her arms. "Darling, are you going to be alright? It's only a movie."

But you knew better. Your mother didn't know that I will forever be the idea of your dog. I will be the pair of golden eyes in your flashlight's beam. I will be the dance of claws on the red oak floor, the almost imperceptible tail-thumping as you walk into your great late-night-fire-lit room, my bed at the right of your leather wing-back rolled arm chair, my portrait, collar, and bowl centered on the green marble mantle piece.

And when the time comes, have no fear. All you have to do is stretch out your hand. I'll be there waiting for you, all cold nose, warm heart and ears—on the other side of the darkness.

# American Gothic

There was only one drop of blood
at the signing, so imperceptibly
small, even the lawyers, who were trained
to smell blood across a room, sat
oblivious.
        The drop rose
out of the fingernail of his right
thumb, trailed down the pen, disappearing
into the ink. It was nothing, really, much
less than the sting of a bee.
His wife
felt a mosquito bite, but an hour
later when the two youngsters walked
their very own fields, he could see
the damp red tracks following them
through the orchard grass.
For a moment, her eyes came off
his implacable face and took in the western sun.
It's all so beautiful, she told him.
He agreed, his hand
moving to the smooth neckline
of her white satin dress. Dragonflies
circled fifty feet above their heads. Dragonflies
so thick you could climb your way
higher than the tree-top
ionosphere. You could rise
up. You could do a planetary
float until it's all

green, black, and blue.

"You're so beautiful," he said.

They stood frozen just like
that until the light
went down into evening
rising moon, into sweet crushed
hay, into sweet crushed hay
thick on their backs.

The next morning they started to find blood
everywhere: the cracked
steering wheel of his antediluvian
truck, the smooth hickory handle
of his splitting maul, her genealogically
acquired pie plates. Even a thin pink
patina floated on their prize-winning
French fingerling mashed potatoes.

Blood showed up particularly well on mail
from the town clerk, the state and federal
government. Blood even trickled
out of her three hundred thread count
Egyptian cotton sheets.

In fifty-three years they ran seven bloody
black dogs and kids while blood
oozed out of plane tickets for the family
life-changing trip to the Indian

sub-continent, art history
text books for the elite
metropolitan eastern college, certified
organic mesclun mix from the town
cooperative grocery.

They built their low-impact farmstead
off-grid on a high ledge of land, and built it
out of earth, sand, clay, and blood—a red
ochred garden wall, spring house, a magnificent
round utopian red barn.

Still, there were giant Cinderella
Pumpkins, bears in the berry
patches, and garlic
the size of a fat man's fist.
Sometimes
he'd open his arms to all that milk and honey.

"I don't know if I'm half-full or half-
empty," he'd say with his abbreviated
grin.

But he was way past half-empty.

She ran out of blood first and got carried
out of the kitchen, still in her lacy apron, past
an entire conflagration of square
sponge cakes, apple sauce, and bean salad.
He lasted another ten years, annually cutting

over ten cords of wood right up until
he sounded like metal on metal when he walked
across the wide pine floor. Instead of wasting
a good tool, they pried the pitch fork
out of his hard busted knuckled hands, and then
draped his blue work shirt and John
Deere hat over the tractor seat in holy

agricultural memoriam. A big
fried chicken and pork chop party, two
kegs, plus some very interesting Australian
Pinot Noir, fiddles, ancient
circle dances, bloody chest high hay
swinging in the late July evening breeze.

It's the way it works.

# underground

<u>adjective</u>

un·der·ground ˈən-dər-ˌgraund : being, growing, operating, or situated
below the surface of the ground

# October, 1972: Peak

" The world may be mean, but people don't have to be, not
if they refuse."

—Colson Whitehead

You should have seen me smile when I heard the power downshift. Seconds later, a purring white cloud of a car was idling right next to me and my soaked-through pack. In the dark pelting rain, a big guy jumped out of what I thought was the passenger door, and tossed my pack into a cavernous trunk. He hustled back and pointed to the other side of the car. My numb hands fumbled with the door handle until he opened it from the inside. The door opened backwards.

"British Engineering," he said.

Everything smelled like a tack room and something right out of the oven, but when he switched on the dome light, I just froze.  The entire interior was plush crimson leather and bright wood dash. He started to laugh.

"It's all right. Not a problem. It's a lot better in here than out there."

That laugh was definitely in the sublime category. No joke. He sounded like Santa: a real "Ho, ho, ho." I couldn't help but smile.

I slid into the red glow, and fumbled the door closed behind me. "So cold," I managed to say.

He ho, ho, ho'ed again and reached down to crank up the heater. It blew hard into my chest and face. I closed my eyes for a second. Heaven, I thought. This is what heaven must feel like.

"Here. Try one of these." He shoved something into my stone cold right hand. When I opened my eyes, I could see that it was a monster brown cookie. I could barely get it to my face. I got the thing to my mouth, tried to chew, and then bowed my head.

"That's it," he said. "Talk about a miracle. These things are like a sacrament with every bite."

I tried to nod, and then a real miracle happened. I bit down hard on that thing and chewed. When I did, everything came into focus. I was sitting next to a guy who looked like someone had shoehorned him into the driver's seat, and immediately it became obvious: yes, some people look like their dogs, but this guy looked like his car. He was wearing a white double-breasted trench coat with epaulets, and he had one of those Irish tweed newsboy hats from the 30s planted on backwards. His wide, jowly face was red with a 100% grin—and then I landed on it: his face looked like a big fleshy ham wearing black glasses. He pulled out another monster cookie from the box on his lap and turned it in his pink banana fingers.

"Mildred. She gave me an entire *dozen.*

He stressed the word dozen and let out that elevated laugh.

"Don't hold back now."

I took another bite of mine, and then realized how delicious they were. The rain drummed on the long white hood.

"I have died and gone to heaven," I said.

He studied his cookie for a moment.

"Milly should know this."

He raised his head, looked out the windshield into the downpour, set his cookie on top of the box, and then stuck out his big, pink banana fingers. We shook.

"I'm Jack Mahoney, and what in the world are you doing hitchhiking on a night like this. Good god, it's almost midnight.  No mortal soul is out on the road tonight."

I told him to call me James. I don't know why I said it. I think I was just trying the name out, or maybe I wanted to be someone else for a while. I always went by

Jim—even Jimmy—and then I told him the shortest possible version of the story I had been using all day, how I had wanted to see the Vermont peak foliage during our fall break at Penn State.

"Crazy. Down there everything is still green—only a hint of color. I couldn't believe it coming into Vermont. It's got to be peak."

He nodded. "Most definitely. And you have to breathe it in like it's your last breath. I've done exactly that. Immerse yourself, my young friend. Internalize. When it's peak, you can taste it. Peak has a flavor. Try it."

I took a deep breath, held it, and tasted nothing. My entire body started to tremble, but I nodded in agreement anyway. I gave him a slurry, teeth chattering account of how I had left State College, PA at 5:00 A.M. and got ride after incredible ride—a trucker going into New York state, a professor took me to Springfield, a VW van full of hippies took me into Vermont, a logger with his two coon dogs into St. Johnsbury, and then a Lyndon State student dropped me off here around 7:00 at this pull-off on RT 5 where my luck ran out.

"It wasn't raining then, but as soon as he left, it started to drizzle."

"Well the good lord is really emptying his bladder now, " Jack said.

"Welcome to Vermont: one minute you're bathed in French Impressionistic foliage, and the next, you're dying of hypothermia."

He chomped on his monster cookie.

"Where are you headed on this frog washer of a night?"

Again, I tried to keep it simple. "Montreal. I have some friends there. Thought I'd cross at Troy."

He nodded enthusiastically, switched off the dome, and rested his left hand on the shift lever.

"Yes. Troy. Perfect. Unbelievable. Exactly where I'm headed."

I leaned back into the red leather as he eased into the road.

The heater was trying hard to blow-dry me, and I could feel my hands and feet again. I took another bite of my monster ginger-molasses and became hypnotized by the lite-up gauges on the dash.

"This car is a wonder. What is it?"

"You're asking all the right questions. This is a 1936 Jaguar 2.5 liter four door Sports Saloon that my Irish Aunt Judy gifted me upon my graduation—and to drive it is pure joy. I tried for the roadster, but we compromised. Aunty Judy demanded that I have a car with dignity. I drive it very little—only on Sunday night when I'm all through with work for the week to celebrate 'All things bright and beautiful, All creatures great and small.'"

I couldn't keep my eyes off the lite-up dashboard. Jack's face beamed in the light.

"So what's your draft number?"

The question hung in the air for a long moment, and then slowly parachuted down between us. I don't know why I thought I could fool anybody. Young men had been lining up at the Canadian border since 1965. All day my story was that I was going to visit my best friend at Lyndon State and take in Vermont peak foliage. But he knew. The dashboard light glowed on his smiling face.

"21," I said.

He power up-shifted on a straightaway. In the headlights, red and yellow leaves were falling along with the heavy rain.

"Might as well be one. So, let me guess. You don't want to kill anybody, but everybody else wants you to, starting with Richard Nixon, right down to your father and your girlfriend."

He took a big bite out of a fresh cookie, set it down on the box on his lap, and then slapped his belly with his pink banana fingers.

"Jesus, I can't stop with these things. Got to drop a few pounds. "

He slipped it into fourth and caught a little rubber on the wet road.

"Continental tires. Grabbers. Love 'em. I understand that Pirelli is a good tire, but I'm sticking with stock for the time being. And your father said something like 'You are no longer my son.' He probably used the word 'coward'."

A sign on the black road announced the town of Burke, and as we drove through, not a single light was on. In the headlights, the church steeple clock read fifteen minutes after midnight.

"A lot of these folks are my customers. Ford country. Do you know what Ford stands for?"

He took a generous bite and waited for a reply.

"Henry Ford?" I said with a shoulder shrug.

"Nope, it's an acronym: Found on road dead. Nice people, but they have to get to know you first. They'd never give a guy like you a ride."

The posted sign read 25MPH in black bold. He pointed at it and let out one big 'Ho'.

"I'm pretty good with all the commandments except the eleventh: Thou shall not rip through Burke at sixty. Hold on. This mile-long down hill stretch out of town is absolutely saintly. Oh yeah."

The deep throaty exhaust rose to a full scream, and we jumped from sixty to seventy. A gust of wind came up and scattered the leaves in front of us, and I was pushed deeper into the red leather. The front end started to tremble. Faster. His smile went extra-wide 110% jowly. He powered down at the bottom of the hill and took the sharp left turn in a four wheel drift. The Jag dug in and clung to the wet road, straightening perfectly. It all happened too fast to be scared.

"Where in the world did you learn how to drive like this?"

He ho, ho, ho-ed and pushed the stick into fourth.

"It's one of the things I was born to do. How about you?"

I don't know why I was so honest with him, but I was. I told him that I was all about writing, and if I could write one good story during my life, it would be enough. I told him that I loved my classes, that I wanted to be a professor and lead students to Higher Ground. I told him that I felt like the classroom was a church, the library was a temple, and I told him I wanted to get my hands dirty, too, grow my own food, live off the land, plant my own flag. I told him that I had read Gandhi and was taken to a better place with 'We but mirror the world'. I told him that like Ghandi, I wanted to be a humanitarian—give something back. I told him I needed to serve, and not just hang around soaking up heat. The strangest thing was that it was all coming out of my mouth for the first time like a true confession. He listened, eyes focused on the road, big jowly smile.

We broke the 11th commandment ripping through Burke. We broke the 12th., 13th., 14th., and 15th. ripping through Sutton, Barton, Browningsville, and Coventry respectively. He actually slowed down when we pulled into Troy. He pulled up next to the St. Vincent de Paul Church and cut off the engine. He picked up the cookie in his lap and chomped in the darkness. He addressed the pouring rain.

"St. Vinny was a good guy.  Champion of the poor.  It's easy to champion the poor around here. That's all we have."

He shook his head and stared at what remained of his monster cookie.

'The woman who made these things is an angel, but if I keep eating them, I'll be on the wrong side of the dirt. If you're going to make a difference as a humanitarian professor and writer and become a Moses of the people—and make no mistake, that's your intention—you're going to need an education. Am I right?"

I stared at the church and didn't say anything. There was a lone light shining on the steeple. The church was vanilla bean ice cream white with big red double doors and trim. Jaguar colors, I thought. He continued.

"Of course you can be a humanitarian without a degree. The boy scout who helps an old lady across the street is a humanitarian, you could be a mop man for Sister Teresa, but your intention is to work at a cerebral level on the Maslowian pyramid."

I told him I didn't know who either of those people were.

"You will. Abraham recently died. His teacher is a good guy, too. Harry Harlow still lives. Sister Teresa will become a saint in your lifetime."

Crimson and amber maple trees lined the street. If it wasn't for the cold, pelting rain, it would be paradise. I spoke to his shadow.

"I've registered as a Conscientious Objector, but it hasn't been granted. I've had my physical. I could be called up any day now. It's either jail or Canada. I'm just taking care of business."

"Good thinking staying out of jail."

He cleared his throat and brought the car to life. The dash lights illuminated his face. He was smiling and chewing. Even his chew was comical. My grin could have matched his.

"James, a third option does exist. What if I told you that Nixon will end the draft on January 27 of next year. By doing so, he thinks he's going to undermine the peace movement in the country. He thinks everyone will embrace him as a righteous man. He thinks affluent youths will stop protesting the war once their own probability of having to fight in it is gone. But mysterious and clandestine forces are afoot. As a result, what if I tell you that he'll resign the presidency in disgrace, and right before the helicopter takes him off the White House lawn— he'll flash double peace signs before disappearing into the belly of the beast. And you won't be called up. Nobody will. You could be Stay-In-School Moses and prepare yourself for that high road, and if you want to be a humanitarian, you can be a humanitarian. You have my personal guarantee on the matter. James, for god's sake, we need humanitarians.  I wouldn't be so enthusiastic if you told me you wanted to make 150 K selling robotic vacuum cleaners."

He revved the engine and smiled a little at the throaty sound.

"Dual carburation. The trick is to get them working in unison. Not unlike life in general. Now, right around back there are some bulkhead doors that go to the church basement. They're open. You just need to pull hard, and at the bottom of the steps, there's half a brick stuck in the right hand corner, under which you will find a key. Once you open the door, immediately on the right you'll find a light switch. You'll also find a stocked fridge, bathroom, shower, and a small bunk in the office. Make yourself at home."

A generous gust of wind came up and rocked the Jag a little.

"I can't do that, Jack. I can't break into a church and use their stuff. That might be my 11th. Commandment."

He ho, ho, ho'ed, and chomped the last of his cookie. He was shaking his head slightly in the dashboard light.

"The church is for the people, not the other way around."

"Still, I just. . . . "

He cut me off.

"If anyone gives you trouble, say Frere Jacques gave you his blessing."

He revved the engine and raised his right hand above the steering wheel. He was holding a fresh monster ginger-molasses in his big pink fingers.

"Lord, be gracious to this young Moses of the People and bless him and make Your face shine upon him. Yes, James. I'm the local priest."

If he had slapped my face, I would have been less surprised.

"I thought you were the local mechanic."

His smile spread to all-jowl, and he pointed to a small white garage at the end of the church parking lot.

"That's where I cure the metallic crippled and lame, Monday through Saturday.

He started to open the door on his way to the trunk, and then looked back at me.

"Here, take this for Montreal." A crisp, pink $20 Canadian materialized in his left hand. "And if you run into Milly, tell her I've been thinking about her."

I gave it a good sprint across the church lawn towards the bulkhead. When I turned to give him a wave, there was nothing on the street but swirling leaves.

In my dream, the yelling in the distance was getting closer and closer, and then I felt a thump on my chest and then another. When I finally awoke, a broom handle was floating over my face. She could have been Boudicca's red-haired mother. She was ready to sack London, and I was at the city gate.

"Give me any trouble, and I'll send you to heaven on the next express.

What kind of low life breaks into a church? You're in a league of your own, Mister. I bet you're drunk. I bet you stole the sacramental wine. The police are on their way."

She punched me again in the chest with the broom handle. She punched hard, and it hurt. I told her that I didn't break in—that I had opened the door with the key. Her face was as red as her hair.

"Liar. The hell you did. Who told you about that key?"

"Frère Jacques."

At that moment, I learned about the power of words. Night turned to day.

Boudicca transformed into Snow White, or almost. She did manage to hit me one last time with her broom, but it was just a tap. I told her everything—how he had come out of nowhere in that white Jaguar—a big chubby guy in a white trench coat, hat on backwards. She stood frozen until I got to the part about the cookies. Then, the tears started falling.

"Look," I said. "I'm so sorry. I had no idea he was the local priest. I would have never come here. His idea. Said his name was Jack Maloney, but if anyone questioned me, tell them Frere Jacques said it was OK."

Her hands tightened on the broom handle, and I thought I was going to get it again. It took me that long before I thought to ask.

"Are you Milly?"

She nodded and kept her eyes on my face, walked over to the wall and grabbed a framed photo.

"Is this the man?"

Even during the candlelight Christmas mass, dressed in vestments, his face looked like a ham with black glasses. He was, of course, smiling, probably getting ready to 'Ho, ho, ho.'

She slowly sat down in a throne-like red leather chair, but her hands were still wrapped around that broom handle.

"He told me, 'Tell Milly I've been thinking about her.'"

I thought it was something she would want to hear, but she let go of the broom, put her face in her hands, and then looked back at me, first Boudicca, then Snow White.

"Jack was with us for a little more than two years. He said four Masses every Sunday, starting here at Vinny's, then Barton, then St. Elizabeth's in Lyndon, ending his day at St. John's in Saint Johnsbury. Afterwards, he'd go driving, tearing up and down the roads in that Jaguar. Every Sunday I'd send him off with a box of cookies that I'd leave right here at this table. Ginger-molasses were his favorite. I'd pack a baker's dozen, extra-large to fit into a large man's hands.

I thought she was going to cry again, but it turned into a high-pitched laugh. It must have been a great combination with that low ho, ho, ho.

"I know," I said. "Monsters. I had one. But Milly, what about the cops?"

Another high-pitched laugh.

"I just said that. Old women know who to call for back-up."

Twenty minutes later, I was sitting at the big hard wood table. She had a pile of eggs and blueberry pancakes in front of me, and I was doing a good food disappearing act while she spoke.

"Jack was sent to us in 1936, and showed up in a brand new white Jaguar. The car was a gift from his rich Irish aunt who wanted him to have dependable, respectable transportation. Somehow, he was able to talk her into that four door Sports Saloon. The car was a gift for graduating from the seminary."

"Yes, I heard about some of that."

"For those two years, you would have never known we were in a Depression. Yes, nobody had any money, but the community turned into a family. I taught at the Troy School. One room, eight grades. He served four churches. And that man could fix anything. Carpenter, plumber. Gifted mechanic. Everybody's car, truck, or tractor went in and out of that shop. That man re-roofed half of Orleans County—and had a gang of people helping him that included old men, old ladies, children, and dogs. He referred to them as the 'choir'—as in 'The choir will meet Saturday morning at 8:00 A.M. to button-up the Charbonneau place for winter.' He renovated this entire basement with scrounged materials. He cut in the windows, plastered the walls, brought in this wide pine floor from a dilapidated farm house."

I took it in for the first time. The red Oriental rug made it feel like a farmhouse parlor.

"He wanted the kids of Troy to have a good place to meet. They caught him asleep right down here in this very same red leather chair once before Sunday School and started calling him Frere Jacques."

"Wait," I said. "As in '*Dormez vous*'?"

She nodded. "One fall night he was racing home and went off the road north of Burke. There's a long downhill, followed by a sharp left turn. He slid on the wet leaves, and over he went, down the rocky bank and into the river. When they pulled that Jaguar out of the river, it didn't even look like a car. The entire Northeast Kingdom was in mourning."

I stopped in the middle of full chew. My hands started shaking, and I dropped my fork right on top of pancakes. For a second, I felt dizzy and grabbed onto the table.

Milly went to the sink and started washing dishes. There were beautiful cupboards above it made out of cherry and tiger maple. The counters were a mosaic of white and green marble slabs she said Jack had found on the railroad bed.

'Then, it started happening. Maybe once a year in the fall, somebody would see a white Jaguar scream by, or somebody from away would break down in the middle of nowhere, and he'd appear with his toolbox. But for a number of years, I thought he was finally gone—off to where spirits go, but you brought him back. He must have thought you were in trouble. Are you?"

"Never colder in my life," I said. She didn't need to know everything.

I tried sipping my coffee, but it ran down my chin and onto my shirt. Whatever he was, he was real. I had shaken his hand. I had eaten one of his cookies.

She almost smiled, kept staring at my face, then lifted her left hand. She was wearing a gold band with a large green stone. It matched her eyes.

"He said he broke his 16th Commandment for me: 'Thou shall not fall in love with the Troy School teacher.' I've told everyone that this ring belonged to Frank Ryan, a nice young man who left town in 1936 to fight with the Abraham Lincoln brigade in Spain. We had been friends since we were kids, but Frank wanted something more—and I didn't.

He was killed at the Battle of Teruel in January, 1938, a couple of months after Jack went off the road.  That's when I started wearing this ring. I told everybody it was Frank's. Sometimes death makes everything easy. I wear Jack's grandmother's emerald wedding ring, but not the years of public rebuke that would have come with it. He said maybe we could find a way to be together. Maybe we have. You know, we never even shook hands."

She took a sip of coffee, and glanced at her watch.

"This time of year just breaks my heart. Yes, I'm the volunteer custodian at St. Vinny's every Monday, but I'm also the principal of the Troy School. We have nine rooms now, a gym-auditorium, and a staff of twelve. I have to be at my desk in twenty minutes. Monday is a school day for some of us."

She was still training her green x-rays on me. I reached for my back pocket and grabbed my wallet.

"Look. Milly. I need to donate to the church."

I pulled out the rosy-pink Canadian twenty and handed it over. When she took it, her eyes got big and her soft smile went schoolmarm hard.

"Where in the world did you get a 1935 Princess Elizabeth twenty dollar Canadian bill, Mister?"

"When I told Jack I was headed for Montreal, he put it in my hand."

She went Snow White again, shook her head, and passed it back to me.

"No." She threw her head back and laughed. "Jack called these Shirley Temples, said Princess Elizabeth's portrait on them looked like the movie star. Every time he'd return from Montreal from buying sacramental wine, his pockets would be full of these. He never told me how he got them, but he did say, 'Nobody ever looks in the priest's trunk'. For weeks afterwards, people in four parishes were eating meat."

Then she x-rayed me again. She took her time. I just sat in front of her. There was nowhere to hide.

"I want you to hold on to this bill. You're going to need it where you're going."

Apparently, there was no fooling the men and women of Troy, Vermont.

Troy had received four inches of snow that night, and I would have had frozen feet hitchhiking in my sneakers if Milly hadn't given me those vintage size twelve galoshes with the explanation, "He always hated these things. He said they interfered with his driving."

I walked up to the border crossing. The guard was talking to a milk truck driver and waved him through. When the guy saw me and my huge Kelty pack, he rolled down his window.

"I'm going to St. Johnsbury. Would that help?"

By 11:00 P.M., I was reading *Huck Finn* in the Penn State library.

As it turned out, everything Frere Jacques said came to pass. Nixon ended the draft on January 27,  1973. I found out later that my call-up was scheduled for February 2. By '74, he got Watergated, resigned, and then departed from the White House lawn by helicopter, flashing a sunny smile and double peace signs before disappearing into the political ether. I finished my undergraduate degree at Penn State. I learned who Abraham Maslow was, and then by a series of other miracles, I found my way to graduate school and then teaching jobs around the world—in China, Portugal, India—and then I landed a job at a little college in northern Vermont of all places, where I've been selling tickets to Higher Ground. Frere Jacques saw the future all right. In 2016 Mother Teresa even became a saint.

I've kept that 1935 8-year-old Princess Elizabeth $20 dollar Canadian in my wallet for over fifty years now, and every fall, I take it out and see Jack all over again: white trench coat, Irish newsboy hat on backwards, black glasses on his big smiling ham face. I have no doubt that he's out there breaking some double digit commandments; ho, ho, ho-ing on the downhill north of Burke; cradling a box of ginger-molasses cookies on his lap. If you're in enough trouble, don't despair: he's coming for you. The drizzle has turned to downpour, the temperature has taken a dive and is on its way to snow. Bright leaves are swirling steeple high in the late night air. Take a deep breath and immerse yourself from the inside out. Taste it. It's Peak.

# Joey

Everytime you heard his voice, you'd see his face, like it would appear in the air in front of you. And it wasn't just his face: you'd get the whole long and skinny man, blue overalls, a nautically inspired blue and white striped short sleeved t-shirt, sweat-soaked blue cowboy bandanna around his neck, wide brimmed straw hat with a crow tail feather sticking straight up in the air, black rubber boots. When he wasn't talking, which was seldom, you'd see Marcel Marceau miming a farmer.

When I heard the ring, I dashed down the long dark hall to the phones in the dorm/barracks lobby in my version of pajamas: a Mr. Natural t-shirt and Black Watch plaid boxers. The phone was cold in my hand, and I couldn't find my voice. I had left most of it at the house party where I had been singing and playing fiddle most of the night for beer drinkers and contra dancers. It was the beginning of a week off for Thanksgiving with an early snow storm warning,  and everybody was howling. Something close to a hello with a question mark came out. The line was always full of static. It was part of the joke that we all had about the place. The dorm was a former barracks built during WWII, and we all said the phone line was still in the fight.

"It's Joey."

I should have known. It was Joey's ring:  the big clock on the back wall read 5:30.  Saturday morning.  No one else would have had the presence of mind to call a college student at that time. Without doubt, Joey had been up for at least a good two hours, pressing apples and making cider doughnuts for the Christmas tree rush that would start around 8:00. After twenty years of his eccentrically brilliant marketing, the people of southern Maine were well-trained: they were lining up at his front gate to reserve their certified organic Christmas trees *before* Thanksgiving, and nobody in the Kittery-Portsmouth area could live without Joey's uniquely marketed maple syrup. The guy sold it in Sweet Old Men and Sweet Old Women bottles. Some years ago, Joey bought Pinocchio bottles and couldn't keep them in stock. All were the ultimate holiday gifts. After my brother Jake's death, since I was thirteen, I had become Joey's sole employee, and he couldn't wait for my return for the holidays. I couldn't either. He ran his entire farm on hard work, focus, invention, improvisation, and frugality. He told me once that four cents out of the first nickel he ever made was still in The Piscataqua Savings Bank. And he was cheerful. You never saw him without a smile. The day after a northeaster took half of his barn roof off, he was up there singing while I muscled up cedar shakes. We covered "Spanish Ladies," "Haul Away, Joe," "Blood Red Roses."

The whole day was call and response, and I didn't feel like I was even working until I got on my bike to ride home. I barely made the three miles, and when I finally arrived, my mother asked me how I had lost my voice.

"Joey," I told her. She went wide-eyed, nodded, turned down mouth. She hurriedly put some fresh water in the kettle to make her famous cider vinegar, ginger and honey drink that brings back vocal cords.

Joey didn't think I heard him.

"It's Joey."

I told him that he was coming through loud and clear. I told him that my Maine-bound Greyhound was leaving State College at noon headed for turkey–"that's the animal, not the country"–but with the snow storm, there was no telling when I was going to see the ocean again.

"Joey, as soon as I get there, I'm yours. Can't wait to charge into the barricades."

And then there was that awkward silence. Immediately, I thought it was part of my mother's awkward silence phone call from a couple of weeks ago. There was almost a tone of formality in her voice.

"I'm calling to let you know that I've been seeing Joey Kline."

And you'd think a twenty year old would have had the sophistication to understand what she was trying to say, but I didn't. By then she had been divorced for seven years. I just made it harder for her. I told her that I, too, had been seeing Joey Kline all my life. I told her that Joey has been an example of big-hearted generosity of deed and spirit, that his farm has been an island of good and right action in the world for my entire memory. I told her that Joey could have been an American founding father, *sans* slaves, a man who truly believed in inalienable rights for *all*–which means everybody–that he had/has that kind of vision, a true land of the free and the home of the brave vision where everyone has a seat at his home-made reclaimed oak dinner table, which was always piled high with leafy green vegetables, home-made hot sauce inspired bean dishes, and no brown heart attack food. I told her that when I was seven, Joey told me that eating beans doesn't hurt anybody, he told me a man could be a feminist, and I told her, ever since I can remember, Joey never forgot my birthday. When my dracula father wouldn't let me have a dog, Joey bought a black and white English Shepherd, told me it was mine, and kept it for me at his farm with a 24/7 visiting policy. I named that dog, Badger. What made it worse, when I was speaking to her, it felt like there was a big, invisible hand squeezing my throat, but that didn't stop me. I just choked it out.

"When I was seven years old, Joey Kline bought me a dog."

I said it like it was brand new information, like knowing it would be a revelation. She started laughing.

"Don't forget: I was there."

I had more to say.

"When I was in ninth grade, I misused the word "irony." Joey took the time to explain situational irony to me, and I understood it for the first time. We were shearing balsam Christmas trees–which Joey said made the finest tree. 'A fresh cut blue spruce will smell like cat piss. A fresh cut balsam smells like *Nirvana*. Pick one.'

Joey went on to explain that situational irony is when the outcome is opposite the expected outcome.

"Think Jaws. The shark hunter is eaten by the shark. Or better yet, imagine a twenty-four year old son of observant Jews leaving Brooklyn and his family's very lucrative marketing firm on a beat twelve speed bicycle, peddling to Maine, purchasing a broken down farm with his life's savings–a wad of cash he pulls out of his back pocket–and creating a full vegetable/fruit CSA and Christmas tree holiday epicenter where the extended  community creates sacred familial holiday traditions. See, the outcome is opposite the expected outcome, and that, my young friend,  is ironic."

My mother interrupted me.

"You don't seem to understand. Your brother once said that your head was full of bent, rusty nineteenth century cut nails, and that those nails had been pulled out of  dry rotted barn lumber. I'm beginning to think he was right. I'm trying to tell you that Joey Kline is not only our neighbor and family friend. Joey Kline is my boyfriend."

There was an awkward silence, and then we both started laughing. This silence with Joey was equally awkward.

The line went static. It sounded like someone was coughing over distant gunfire.

I hadn't spoken to Joey since my mother's announcement, but I told him that everything was OK. I told him that we were always like family anyway. I told him now it was just more official.

I could hear him fine, but in the background, the line cracked small arms fire again.

"No, Jim. No. Everything is not OK."

Joey's voice had flat-lined. It's not him, I thought. Somebody else. Not Joey.

"Who is this," I said.

The voice spoke again.

"Last night. In your kitchen. We were playing music. I had picked up Bach's *Four Duets for Cello and French Horn,* and Jim, she was playing like she was Jacqueline du Pré in concert–navy blue dress, her long blonde hair flying around her face. Something had taken hold of her. I felt like Bach was in the room, and my part on the horn was fine and chiseled. Can't explain it. I felt like she was carrying me. For a few moments, I had no body. We were tongue and groove–perfect fit, fine stitched. My horn was playing itself."

The line went hollow and echoed just a little. There was the first version of what he said, and then the same words repeated a beat later, but they sounded underwater.

"JoAnn had put a candle on the sill of that wide arched-top ocean-side window, and it made the entire kitchen reflect in the glass. She was playing right next to me, and then in the window. I was reflected in the window, too, looking at her. Outside, five miles away, Whaleback Light was strobing double white every ten seconds, like a man was way out there on the water with an open boat and a flashlight. The windows rattled with a gust of wind, and then she started staring at something, like something had let itself in through the back door."

The hollow sound disappeared, and the voice I knew came back.

"She was staring at something, and moving her head, as if someone was walking across the room, and then stopped right in front of us. She dropped her bow. I grabbed it off the floor and held it up to her, but she was focused straight ahead, her eyes slightly elevated. Her reflection–and mine–filled the glass. Your mother started talking to someone."

On the line, there was a brief burst of faraway machine gun fire, the faint whistle of bombs, and then the line went clear of the echo. Joey sounded like he was standing right in front of me.

"She started to cry. She said, 'I'm sorry. I can't go now. Do you understand? My boy needs me, and I'm not leaving him. Absolutely not.' And then she sat frozen, looking into the window like somebody was speaking to her. A long minute. I almost spoke. I almost reached out, I almost touched her, but she nodded her head, started to smile and let out a laugh. 'Well, OK.' she said. 'OK. If it's going to be like that. That's so beautiful.' She turned to me, laughing, holding her cello. In the candle light, she looked like she was eighteen. She reached out and grabbed my hand, leaned over, inches from my face. 'Joey, it's so beautiful.' I kissed the tears on her face, and when I kissed those tears,  she said, 'Joey, Joey I'm sorry.' Big smile. She put her hand on my cheek. 'I'm so sorry, Joey. I have to go,' and then she slumped into my arms. York had their Cadillac ambulance there in twenty minutes, but she was gone. I didn't need any doctor to tell me she was gone. Jim, your mother died in my arms."

The black phone was cold in my hand, and my fingers felt numb. The line faintly buzzed, whistled and popped. Mortar rounds.

I looked out the dorm window into the black. The all-night overhead light in the lobby turned the window into my reflection, but in back of it, faintly, I could see snow falling. Is that what I look like, I thought. Is that who I am? Am I in a snow dome?

The line crackled with Joey's voice. I looked at my shaking left hand and passed the phone to my right. I couldn't hear what he was saying. When I looked back at the window, my mother was standing there on the outside. She was standing there in her navy blue dress, face pressed up to the glass, her wide blue eyes high-beaming into mine. She stood there for a good ten seconds. She stood there,  and when I reached up to touch the glass with my left hand, she drifted back into the dark. Joey spoke through the distant artillery.

"Jim, I'm leaving now. Gassing up the Power Wagon. Coming to get you. Wally Kinnan the Weatherman says there's eight inches already on the streets of Boston. Two inches an hour. We got ourselves a humdinger, but storm or no storm, I'll lock hubs and be there in eight hours."

In the window, I watched myself answer him.

I told Joey that I'd be ready. Joey told me he was bringing my dog.

# underground

: a clandestine conspiratorial organization set up for revolutionary or other disruptive purposes especially against a civil order

# Strolling Dark Town with Mother

I imagine the principles of soulful
dispatch reversing themselves. I imagine
an inspirational evening fringed with serious
affect. I also imagine I'm quite
cavalier. "May I have this walk? I say
to black air.

          Of course, you agree, and then
the sound of footsteps, a touch on my
shoulder. Christ, I can imagine
anything walking past rambling
congregations of whispering houses. Each
comes with its own
cartoon cat.

          And I sense
you're at ease. You love to walk; you love
town at night; you love cats. So, I easily play
the bright, promising boy—your favorite
amongst all others—my elocution tightening
into hardwood. I even imagine
having something important
to ask you. "Did you actually
love Father." I say, passing a parked
car. "Was I at all entertaining
as a child?"

          But since
communication's at a considerable
impasse, I revert
to apology. I say to a dark door, "I'm

sorry I was brain-dead between
the ages of seven and twenty-one. I'm sorry
I was a social paraplegic."
                          Or maybe
I just imagine I'm sorry. Why, with the way
the years have muddied themselves, you've
become an elegant woman's winning
smile, a cordial stranger, the efficient
hostess who demurely refills a coffee
cup, as if it's just what I
need, just enough, as if you
actually do know something
about me, or I you, or that we're not
really tiny bits of memory
walking disproportionately
into the point at the end of the road.

## Self Portrait with Straw Hat
## (After the Van Goth)

I'd give anything to paint a hug and kiss
just right, and I'd paint them
on me if the mirror would

lie. She says one eye's tired and kind–
the other's mad; neck–thick; nose–
aquiline. She says this town whirls

around like a hundred dog tails
in the wind–turns everyone's cheeks
hollow–sculpts small pointed

minds and chins. Mustache hangs
over upper lip, ear completely
too red, beard trimmed in almost

a straight line. And the hat's
a golden circle of light, the brim
wings out into space, but the crown

falls low on the brow, like it's
entirely too big, or like
there's something it's trying to hide.

# In an Effort to Explain,
# Nancy Takes Us All to Lunch at Rosie's

## (A Play in a Story's Clothing)

Everyone, please understand: my arms are wide open at the very sight of you. I am so happy. Let's present ourselves ensemble, a kindly, beneficent army of rebel irregulars—all blue, of course. A blue army, going into a blue restaurant, in a blue town, in the bluest state, a blue island in a blue sea, and I shall play all three of Charles Dickens's ghosts—Past, Present, and Future—all at the same time, so in the great tradition of Victorian spirits transporting mortals through time, "Bear but a touch of my hand there," you mortals. And I shall be your guide. Whatever it is that you're looking for, I assure you it will be waiting for you at Rosie's Restaurant.

Yes. Listen. The snow is squeaky under foot. Hear the door open in a regal whoosh? You are experiencing that intangible Rosie's quintessence, not happiness—but something beyond ecstasy, so let's pause for three beats and radiate in the warm glow, squeeze each other's arms a little tighter. I'll imagine you're my Heathcliff—or my Catharine. We certainly don't have to be binary: we can just be. You are my guest. Your identity is your choice, and with choice, there's no effort to smile, and honestly, a smile doesn't come close. Rosie's makes me beam. The light is bright but never hurts, so open your eyes wide. In fact, nothing hurts as soon as you step through the bright varnished double oak doors. Let's agree with Jaques from *As You*

*Like It,* that "All the world's a stage,/And all the men and women merely players…." Those doors are our curtain. Our audience awaits. Let's play.

Wait. Pause again under the first eighteenth century two tier fifty candle hand wrought chandelier, gaze upward and drift back to the time when Vermonters arrived at Rosie's by sleigh and the jingling of harness bells. Can you imagine entering the building into all that light? I can see everyone's bright red cheeks that match their red felted mittens, entire families emerging from under buffalo robes. Hear them shout greetings. Hear their laughter as they shed their horses out back under the moonshine.

Now, hold on tight as we approach the exceptional entrepreneur owner-hostess-server, Sarah, whose great, great, great, great grandmother Rosie Benton started the establishment during our American Revolutionary War. Local historians say that Rosie served British officers tea and extra wide slices of Marlborough pie while she gathered intelligence for Ethan Allen and our Green Mountain Boys. Don't you wish we could have known her? It wasn't so long ago. It feels like I have known Sarah for at least as long. Sarah used to Halloween at our house. Sarah played with my daughters.

"Why hello, Nancy." Sarah's smile broadens as we approach her neoclassical birds-eye maple hostess lectern, and my eyes see the little girl in her homemade Wizard of Oz Cowardly Lion costume. "If I only had a heart," she sang out. She actually jumped through the doorway past the tootsie rolls and perched halfway up the stairs. "Twick or Tweat," she shouted, grabbed her tail, used it as a handkerchief soaking up faux lion tears. and then burst into a boisterous bravado. "If I were king of the forest. . . . " I swear, at that moment, that little girl was better than Bert Lahr, who, as you remember, originally played the part. But that was so long ago. Now, Sarah could double for Katherine Hepburn.

"Nancy, welcome back to Rosie's," she says as she reaches out and squeezes my hand.

Now, let your eyes drift to the Hepplewhite glass pastry case that Rosie's uses to display their daily choices of seven homemade desserts, about which I have often wondered.

It's really quite a conundrum. Do you think they use the word homemade literally or figuratively? Does the *pàtissière* actually make all those splendid desserts in the early morning hours at their home, and transports them to this display case in time to greet the earliest Rosie's patrons, who smell of good hay and oiled leather? Or does it merely refer to the care and considerations one would give a homemade dessert? I just know that if any dessert were made by me at my home the major ingredients would be apprehension, anxiety—and largely salted with pounds upon pounds of lack of interest.

We follow Sarah across the exceptionally wide pine boards into the immense post and beam dining room. I am always delighted by the socio-economic diversity of the patronage. There's Rufus Jewett and family brunching on mountains of blueberry pancakes—and all six, including his wife, Marge, and his four beautiful daughters, are completely clad in oak tree camouflage, next to state senator Becca Sharp and her partner, our high school principal, Alice Feldman. There's Keith Emilio, our stellar Chief of Police. Keith is such a fine man, and this morning he's having coffee with his partner, Bill Treadway, the Fire Chief. We have Alex Smith, the builder/singer-songwriter, his beautiful wife, Zelie and two boys—who are no church angels—next to our lawyer, Dick Foote, who is breakfasting with his wife, Ellie, the college women's lacrosse coach. And there's John Elder, the tweed-clad college English professor with our college president, John McDermott, and Damascus Okumbe, the college's ethnomusicologist, who, along with his teaching, directs the college's stellar afro-pop band and our town choir. He taught us all how to sway while singing. Next to Damascus, we have the British mystery writer, Zoë Wright-Neil, her curly haired service dog, Truffa, and her Spanish tycoon industrialist husband, Antonio. House painters Luis Sanchez and Rudolfo Rodriquez are at the table next to Zoë. And of course, Jay Orsini, who commandeers a table in the corner where he works on his novel. Sarah, the kindest big-heart that she is, helps me into my seat, which always has a delightfully happy landing. Please, don't stand on ceremony. Do take a seat.

We exchange greetings with Rufus, who plows snow from my driveway and mows my lawn. His perpetual smile always lands me square on my feet and makes me hold my head up high.

"Out hunting this morning, Rufus?"

"Why, yes, indeed, Nancy. We were lucky enough to tip over a thirty pound tom turkey this morning up in the land of Goshen."

Oh, how I love his delightfully poetic speech. It makes me want to tip over a bit myself.

"Oh, my. Congratulations," I say. "That's marvelous news," However, I do secretly think that it wasn't good news for the turkey.

I wave to the entire room. All wave back with great enthusiasm, all sending us toothy smiles. Becca is in my writing group, Dick handled my divorce from my first husband, and John was my daughter's favorite professor. Unknown to me, she brought my biggest kitchen knife to class when she played Lady Macbeth. "Come, you spirits/ That tend on mortal thoughts, unsex me here/And fill me from the crown to the toe top-full/Of direst cruelty!"

Years later, John very confidentially told me the scene was truly frightening—exactly how Shakespeare intended. Rudolfo and Luis painted our entire house, inside and out, top to bottom, and turned it into a magnificent, sparkling jewel. Both toast me very ceremoniously with their coffee cups.

And then I wave to Jay completely out of protocol, knowing full well that Jay will not give up the time from his novel to wave back.

The Smith boys steal away from their table and stealthily approach, coming at us from two directions. I happen to know that they were pre and post-natally inspired by *Drums along the Mohawk* and *The Last of the Mohicans*. If one is Hawkeye, the other is Leatherstocking.

"I'm a dinosaur, and I'm going to eat you up," roars Archer.

"I'm a dinosaur playing a piano," roars little Rory as he pounds on imaginary keys. Both retreat towards Zelie, whose bright smile also means business. Their library has evidently expanded.

Zoë sends me a very secretive significant smile before supervising her darling, Truffa, who is busy vacuuming the crumbs under everyone's table. Antonio looks on with great regal Spanish implacability.

Sarah gives us our menus, and asks if we'd like to start with a beverage, but we all know that it's cat and mouse. Just don't ask me who's the cat.

I say, chuckling, "Sarah, your wonderful unsweetened ice tea will once again be my choice."

It's OK to chuckle. Let's let the movie of our ordering run, and then sit back and watch.

Stage and screen star Helen Hayes plays me, a woman who has been looking for the very same dish all her life. And for our purposes today, let's imagine a waiter in full regalia, played by Gary Cooper, who as we all know is catnip to women. Coop is slicked back, tuxed, bow-tied, towers over me, and then baritones, "What is your heart's desire, Madam?"

"What's in my heart? What have I always wanted? I'd like a large plate of the balsamic gender equality along with the free-range certified organic full social, political, and economic liberty. And a large piece of your caramelized love and environmental justice on the side, served on a steaming hot bed of whole grain choice." And then let's imagine that I'd pause, look longingly into his big vibrant baby blues, his grand understated blank biscuit face. "And oh, Coop. Do make it snappy. Helen has places to go. "

"Would you like a few minutes to decide," asks Sarah.

She watches me hedge. Sunlight pours through the southern windows. I admire the incomparable craftsmanship of the cherry crown and chair rail molding, the yellow ochre horsehair plaster. There's the double ox yoke, the magnificent ten foot two man crosscut saw, the huge farm-themed quilt—all on display—and of course the prominent gilded framed portrait of Rosie Benton, the establishment's matriarch, where I see Sarah's smile. I wonder if it was that smile that saved the building in 1778 when British officer Major Christopher Carleton burned Middlebury and most of the valley. Was it her grand display of the Union Jack, or was it her generous servings of pepper pot stew, tea, and pie? Regardless, Rosie Benton convinced him that the restaurant was loyalist red. But oh no, Major Carleton. You were very mistaken. Here at Rosie's, even the air is blue.

Helen Hayes speaks. "I think we're ready, Sarah."

Helen's type-cast, in my opinion.

Helen tells Sarah that she'll have the Blue Plate Old Fashioned Vermont Thanksgiving Turkey Dinner Special, which, in my opinion embodies Sojouner Truth, Susan B. Anthony, and Mary Wollstonecraft, all rolled into one grand *entrée*. I do delight in the very thought of it—the very pronunciation.

"Oh yes," says Sarah, nodding, writing on her pad. She smiles a bit wider. "Yes, of course."

And then she comes to the very best part—my choice.

Potatoes baked or mashed? Is there a better vegetable to embody economic equality? A vegetable for all, rich or poor, man or woman—and all genders in between. Today, I think mashed.

Sarah keeps writing, knowing full well that I always choose mashed. I always choose the green beans because green beans are the embodiment of justice: protein and carbohydrates are delivered in a low calorie, delicious, anti-inflammatory reducing fare, and I always choose the Indian pudding over of the stuffing because I need equal representation for the First Nations, and let's face it: is there a better symbol of care, nurturing, generosity, and fairness for all than the turkey. Here at Rosie's everyone receives an equitable, formable, well-gravied slice. And for my house side salad, there is that thing that I love most of all: numerous choice. I see it as self-determination. I'll choose the house raspberry vinaigrette and become who I want to be as a diner. But please understand: I can change it at any time, and know that I'm choosing the Indian pudding just as profoundly as I choose the man I live with.

Now, Please. Please order anything you'd like—anything at all. You're having the chef's salad—hold the croutons now—in an effort to drop weight? Absolutely wonderful. And unsweetened ice tea, as well? Excellent.

Sarah knows, but goes through the questions as if they are critical to the state of the Union, the Magna Carta, the Declaration Of Independence, or Mina Loy's "Feminist Manifesto."

And I do my Helen Hayes, or does Helen do me? One of us answers Sarah's questions, yes, I think, as Helen did in her role as *Mary of Scotland.*

This is where, my mortal friends, I hold my hand against my heart.

"What's happening," you ask?

"Yes. The dreadful thing. Oh, dear."

My friends, touch my hand. Our stage will go black for a moment, but do not be alarmed. Upon illumination, you can see that we've left the restaurant behind, and we are now in the blue hospital, outside the blue town, in the bluest state. Come along. There's room for everyone.

"Happening again?" the cardiologist asks.

"Yes, Dr. Rodney," I tell him. "Yes. I'm in mid-sentence, and the next moment I'm Gene Krupa at Carnegie Hall, and Benny Goodman has just asked for my drum solo. My heart is literally a barrel of monkeys."

I watch Dr. Rodney mouth and nod the name Gene Krupa as he writes on his pad. He does the same for barrel of monkeys. A smile spreads across his puppy belly face.

"Since the oral medication had absolutely no effect on the fibrillation, I've ordered an IV."

Oh Dr. Rodney, you are such a blue-eyed boy. First, I don't want the IV: I want the Blue Plate Special.

Do you know you're going to turn me into Emily from *Our Town*. Before the day is done, I'll be sitting in my chair at the graveyard. Dr. Rodney, for you I will recite from Emily's goodbye monologue. Will you "look at me one moment like you really saw me? Can't you see me? I'm right here in front of you." Can't you see that I'm an ancient, delicate, dehydrated hot house flower? Can't you understand that I have Rosie's unsweetened ice tea running through my veins, and that once the IV goes in, I go out. Dr. Rodney, I'm asking you, can't we, 'just for a moment be together. Just for a moment be happy? Let's look at one another.' "

And now, dear friends, let's look significantly and conspiratorially at each other. Yes. That's it.

Dr. Rodney, I chose The Blue Plate Old Fashioned Vermont Thanksgiving Turkey Dinner, not you, and not the great suffering you'll later serve my family, not to mention my friends here who chose the Chef's Salad.

Which is really at the center of my question, and that is, and I've been wanting to propose this for quite some time to Sarah, mortal friends. Do you think Rosie's should advertise as a *feminist* restaurant—because in essence, that's what it is. Rosie's gives every single one of its patrons full equality and opportunity, regardless of their gender identity—and the choices are vast and various. Rosie's gives everyone access to their very top shelves: there is no glass ceiling of any kind. Do you fully understand that there is even self-determination in the salad dressing. You can choose one of *seven* and your salad can become anything you want. OK, I've said that, but there's even an eighth choice: no dressing at all, which is quite edgy if you think about it. All that nude lettuce in the dining room. That sounds like sexual freedom to me. Regardless, at the center, the Blue Plate Old Fashioned Vermont Thanksgiving Turkey Dinner exemplifies a woman's right to choose. Choice, Dr. Rodney, encircles the very fiber of my being. It's what makes us grand as a society. A people. A nation. Would I rather be here with you, or would I rather be gazing up at the two tier fifty candle chandelier swinging from the apex of Rosie's eighteenth century post and beam dining room? That's called a rhetorical question. And what happens when you take away a woman's right to choose, Dr. Rodney? Do we just shrug our shoulders and say, "Oh, well, perhaps next time, or perhaps some day my daughters will realize this inalienable right? Perhaps we'll just sit here interminably with our knees tight together, hands folded, posture of a ballerina? No, Dr. Rodney, without choice, as you will soon see, we die.

But forward we go. You're a celebrated, golden boy summa cum laude heart specialist, and I'm a 94 year old great-grandmother. Do we need to discuss equality? Someone, please, hand me Emily's farewell monologue. Is this where I say, "Goodbye World"? Are you playing a knight in shining armor, Dr. Rodney? Are you my *El Cid*. Am I a damsel in distress? Do you think you're going to save me? OK, OK, everyone *tells me* to take the IV, but a group of women would have seen that I was a dehydrated hot house flower. A group of women would have talked about it. *That's what we do.* A group of women would have known my blood pressure would disappear. What was it, Dr. Rodney? 25 over nothing?

My friends, touch my hand. The stage will go black for the count of three, but all will be well, and upon re-illumination, it's Sarah!

Desserts? Well, of course. What do I want? I certainly don't want the helicopter ride to the University of Vermont Hospital. I suppose the view is stunning, our magnificent lake on one side and the jaw-dropping mountains on the other. But truthfully, Dr. Rodney, even if I had been conscious and not on life support, I would have closed my eyes. Along with everything else, this hothouse flower in front of you has vertigo.

What would I like, Sarah asks? All of Rosie's Blue Plates come with a choice of all seven desserts, but Helen Hayes happens to know that the flourless double chocolate cake which arrives *à la Mode* with local *homemade* Jersey-cow vanilla ice cream is "over the rainbow." Regardless, let's allow Sarah to describe the others. I listen like Mary of Scotland. They all sound so wonderful, each one a "Road Not Taken." And once again, I do lament that I am but "one traveler." Do you think Mary knew how it was all going to end? I do, Dr. Rodney.

"Just lie down a moment, and you'll administer the IV?"

OK, Dr. Rodney. But first, please hand me the script. I'll be Martha Scott on Broadway in 1938. I read the reviews when I was eleven years old. Do you know that *Our Town* won the Pulitzer? And when Martha was done with them, there wasn't a dry eye in the house. However, this time, Dr. Rodney, I'm going to get my chance. You're going to let me say, "Goodbye. Goodbye, Middlebury, VT. Goodbye Unitarian Church. Goodbye equal pay for equal work. Goodbye iced coffee, Royal Tyler Theatre, the touch of books. Goodbye my own writing. You sustained me all my life. Goodbye Ladies Lunch with my three beautiful granddaughters. Goodbye my dear, dear husband. Goodbye Natural Foods Co-op. Goodbye Christmas morning, apple cider, and birthday cards with large personal checks. Goodbye Amelia, my precious Maine Coon cat. Goodbye my four wonderful children and my seven grandchildren and my great-grand baby boy, and all my great-grand babies on the way. Goodbye my unrelentingly eccentric and wonderful family in all of its marvelous iterations and extensions. As Walt Whitman declared, you are all "multitudes", bottomless and beautiful.

Wait, my mortal friends. I need your help. Let's have a secret understanding: You're going to play the *Our Town* Stage Manager.

"Does anyone ever realize life while they live it every minute?" Emily asks.

And you'll say "No. Saints and poets, maybe." But I'm just one of those. Care to guess? Dr. Rodney, I was a poet who played Jaques from *As You Like It*. Do you understand that when the IV goes in, I will not have a stage. Do you understand? I will have "mere oblivion; Sans teeth, sans eyes, sans taste, sans everything."

Who wrote that? Yes, it's attributed to Shakespeare, and quite frankly, since I'm on the way out and no scholar will be able to aim their ire, let me clarify my position: I'm not convinced. I'm just not convinced William Shakespeare was The Bard. That's scandalous? Well, we'll see. Dr. Rodney, I think Shakespeare was a woman. The plays are rife with heroine. No, Dr. Rodney. Not the drug. That's heroine with an "E" at the end. Yes, all of this will be revealed to you years after I'm dead, which with your help, will be any minute now. Still, as Mary Wallstonecraft said, "appears to me impossible that I should cease to exist, or that this active, restless spirit, equally alive to joy and sorrow, should be only organized dust."

But dust I will be, Dr. Rodney.

Now, Friends, do not be alarmed. There will be a moment of darkness. Hold tight. Just a moment.

And now, the dining room's lights flash, then dim, and Sarah enters. Our Sarah. My Sarah. Our Friendly Lioness with our dessert, and a single candle burning bright above the mountainous scoop of ice cream. Splendid. Truly rhapsodic.

Rufus Jewett and family stand and applaud, as does Officer Keith and Fire Chief Bill, Becca, and Alice, Dick , Ellie. Professor Elder stands and brandishes a huge kitchen knife in great jest. College president McDermott, Damascus, all four Smiths, Zoë, Truffa, Antonio, Luis, Rudolfo, all stand. And good lord, the entire kitchen staff, lead by the pâtissièr has entered the room, hands clapping together. And of course,

Sarah. She rubs my back. And for a moment, it's nothing short of Independence Day. And then a true anomaly, maybe it's a literary miracle: Jay puts down his pen, looks up from his novel and smiles. Our eyes meet significantly before he disappears again into the words.

I stare into the flame. Dear World, everyone has been so kind. What was I looking for? All these years? To be sure, a group of women would have discussed the matter. A group of women would have carefully weighed all eventualities, considered the greater good. A group of women would have looked at me—and they would have seen me for who I am.

I shall take one bite, hold my breath, and savor the moment, but you've had only the salad. Yes, without doubt, this chocolate cake is beyond measure, but the rest is yours. I've had all I want. It was a wonderful choice, and in the end, choice is all I've ever wanted.

And now, dear, dear mortal friends, touch my hand one last time. And thank you so much for your wonderful company. Bliss is to be your friend. Yes, the stage will go black, but have no fear. This is just the place that Frost talked about where "two roads diverged in a yellow wood." I will go my way, and you will go yours, but there's no need to hurry. Our check has been prepaid, and the coffee at Rosie's has no bottom. However, at this point, do join me, imagine all of us are lined-up across the stage's apron, shoulder to shoulder, holding hands, the lime lights bright on our faces. Imagine, all of us, lifting our eyes to the applause. Now, let's take a bow, ensemble, wave farewell, and I will blow out the candle.

# Saturday Night Radio

> "Don'tcha know that everybody
> Is a radio receiver
> All you gotta do
> Is listen for the call"
>
> "Turn Your Radio On"
> —Albert Buntley

Tonight, you say it's everybody's birthday.
You light candles inside airwaves, send every
bad actor to the roads looking for his

piece of cake. Tonight you promised
the band won't quit. You say, "We're going
to dance all night if you like." I do.

I lean back, turn you and the heat
on high. My car's big, black, and slow, and you
smile back inside the dashboard lights, giggle

move over close. You wrap your words around
me in the pronouncements of love, say it
again, quiet and fine. "Honey, we're going to slow

dance until dawn. Well, that sounds right. I'll
slip my hands inside your warm electric
dress, slide along easy with your loud red shoes.

# Steve's Rules

Play. Play until you feel that little
invisible high-fidelity antennae in your head
bend over backwards, or play until that thing
grows right out of your
skull—until you have your own Radio City
Music Hall between your ears, the horn
getting bully, kicking the Rockettes
right off the stage.
                Play. Play
"Silent Night" under bayberry
candles for your grandmother, and then play
for the church carolers in black
top hats, lambs' wool striped scarves, your
fingers keeping loose under the cold madrigal
harmony and clandestine Kentucky whiskey. Play.

Play as your pals crack their bones on a football
field, play in the garage until 4:00 A.M., play
for a scholarship, for your curly-haired
doughboy professor until he gives you
a fine arts degree.
                  Play for the woman
who will become your wife, listen
to her voice rise in the ensemble, and say
to yourself: Yes, Sir, she's got a set
of pipes.
            Play until the years
unfold themselves into a single

breath of honeymoon air, as you see
her face rise in your sleep, touch
the small of her back, the two of you
tumbling into the night.
                    Play for two
babies, recording contracts, your own
black distributor wire hair going
salty. Play every day.
                    Play
until you lose her
from the moment you exit the oncologist's
office, you lose her.
                    Play
her songs for her every day until someone
else is singing them in the Unitarian
Church, some stringy-haired
woman with a practiced smile and a plastic
rose stuck on the head of her guitar. You
play the church packed so
full of New Millennium Alcotts
and Emersons holding hands
there's only room for your solo, sending
out something hot and true into brittle
thin air. You'd swoon if you could. You'd
swoon; instead
                    you play, feeling that little invisible
high-fidelity antennae in your head
bend into the light. Your fingers
know the way. There will be you and your
boy and girl, graveside, and all those years

feeling the count in adagio, glissando
—triste, and dulce, in a thousand lights, your nappy
hair in your face.
                    There will be you
and your girl and boy, but you know how
to do it right: better stand up
straight at the microphone; get your hands all
over that golden, fire-breathing flugelhorn; throw
your head back into the starry
starry night—and play.

## Letter Home to the Great Beyond

There's an old man and an old
woman who took their two car
garage and made it into one of those
particle board apartments–and it's
where I live now–up in the pointy
middle of nowhere where nothing

consequential happens day
in and day out, so I turn
off the lights sometimes and watch
the moon rise, tell funny
stories for hours, I can't

explain why–who knows, but the old
man whistles most of the time he's
on his feet, and  six kids later the old
woman has one hell of a grin, still
walks like a deer–she's got deer
eyes and legs, seventeen brown-
pantsed grandchildren, five
dogs, seven ponies, three half-tame
ruffled grouse, two black and white
heifers, and of course it's amazing

when the phone rings around here, I
jump up and toss it into the closet and run
out to see the moon instead–I
mean if it's rising over these

hills, and if the night's
still and dark enough, and if
my radio's coming in right and the sky's
deep indigo and Jupiter's coming in
low and bright and the local
dogs aren't barking for ten
minutes, and if there's a little
black ruffle of bird feathers
coming out of the pointy trees, that fat
moon will call out: Hello. Hello
down there–and say
something that sounds an awful lot
like my name. Well, I just
wanted to say thanks. I mean, it's one
hell of a life sometimes, and I really
don't know what I'd do without it.

# underground

adverb

: existing outside the purview of statisticians

# Different Drummer

(For Jake)

"And this too is true: stories can save us."

—Tim O'Brien

This is how it works. It's late-September. The bees are all over the hydrangeas outside our falling apart farmhouse, and bushels of two pound heirloom orange tomatoes are swinging on the vines. My wife returns from the mailbox only to put a photograph postcard in my hand. "All the way from France," she says, laughing, and I put on my magnifiers to zoom in. It takes me a couple beats, and then I get it. Good god, it's the septuagenarian version of Dr. Alan on the aft end of a canal boat, and good god, it's Dr. Hazel. That's Hazel, his wife, toasting the camera. Both think something is hysterically funny. He's presenting a copy of *The Complete Works of Henry David Thoreau*, and he's waving with an ear to ear grin. The note on the other side reads, "After forty-three years of pulling over 12,000 babies out of dark places, we're malt-wormed,  floating through France. Bottomless thanks with Big Love."

My wife, Lesley, who knows how to get to the heart of any matter, hesitates for a moment while she fills up a watering can, slips on her green Wellies, bound for her herb garden.

"So who's Alan and Hazel, and why are they thanking you? You've never mentioned them. They sound like fun."

"It's probably more story than you want to hear," I tell her, and she nods, knowing full well what that means. She's almost out the screen door when she glances at my face, and then comes to a full stop. Three seconds later she's back in front of me with her hand on my cheek.

"Darling, you're crying."

"I am? I'm not crying. I don't cry. You know that. Don't know how." And then I elaborate. Not when my mother died when I was in college. Not when I broke my hand. Broken arm. Fifty-seven bee stings. Middle ear surgery. Wisdom teeth. The tree branch that turned into a Louisville slugger when I was logging. Bucked off. Bit. Stomped on. Caught in the electric fence. She doesn't protest.

"I know," she says, "But you're crying. You're either crying, or the roof's leaking, and it's dripping on your face. Is the roof leaking?"

I tell her that I sure hope not, and she takes her soft hand and rubs my cheek. There's a big wet spot on my t-shirt.

"Maybe you should tell me?" and with that she pushes my boat into a sea of memory and sits down with her tea cup.

I tell her.

I tell her even now, over fifty years later, I can still hear the distant banging rumble. I emphasize the word "fifty" for dramatic effect, and she gives me a faux significant look and nod.

"All you do is talk about the past. Why is this any different?"

I tell her that to truly understand the present, one must take stock of the past. I tell her that I can even see the two ragamuffins on the lost highway holding up their stupid sign, and there I am clutching the handle of my fiddle case. I point to my head.

"There's a movie going on in here. Soundtrack, captions, credits, wranglers–the whole thing."

I tell her in the movie, I'm holding the same grandfather fiddle that lives right in back of my chair. I'm thread worn, forlorn, still smiling for some reason, but I'm not letting go: I'm not setting the instrument down on the cold damp ground. Alan is standing right next to me with his Henry David Thoreau and his famous military flashlight. He's got it clipped on his shirt pocket, reading in the inside-of-a-horse darkness, quoting the author when he sees fit. "I too, want to live deliberately," he says,  and then, whatever it is, crests the hill a couple of hundred yards down the road.

It sure doesn't look like a van. With the custom running lights, it looks like a floating two-eyed smiley face rising out of the foggy dark–and you'd think that would have sent us both to the Ichabod Crane, headless horseman place. We have all the right ingredients. In the far distance, there are pops of lightning from a storm coming our way. A waist-high Sherlock Holmes fog is covering a deserted north country 3:00 A.M. highway. We even have horror movie soundtrack. Deep in the pointy tangle of hemlocks, a barred owl's hooting, "Who cooks for you? Who cooks for you-all?" Regardless, when the cartoon route van pulls up out of the fog next to us and our cardboard sign that reads "Anywhere But Here," we are all smiles. Both of us recognize the song that is trying to escape from its steel prison. We are right in the middle of Ginger Baker's drum solo from the Cream instrumental, "Toad." Alan slides Henry David into his pack, but he is quick to capitalize on the moment, and says it aloud with a laugh in the chilly dark. "It looks like we have been saved by the "different drummer," which, of course, is true. A tall, blonde, long-haired skinny kid rolls open the passenger door, bows, and waves us in.

"Hail to thee, goodly pilgrims, and a valorous michaelmas to thee."

He has a remarkable toothy grin, pointy bearded chin, and he is wearing a Lincoln green cape and one of those triangular Robin Hood hats to match–with a sizable turkey tail feather sticking out of it. In direct opposition, my teeth have been chattering for a good hour, my chin's on my chest, and I can't hold my hands steady, but once we step into the warm bright light, I do feel saved, relieved, at ease–having absolutely no idea what is waiting for us just up the road.

Jumping into the van is a little like jumping into the ocean: we are in an entirely different world, and I'm not quite sure we are the right animals. Towards the back end, tucked under a rack of velvety coats and broad brimmed hats, is a very care-fully stowed Ludwig drum kit, but everything else looks like it is medieval Britain. Attached to the ceiling are six English longbows, and tucked into the back right corner is a secured quiver of arrows. A massive, ornate wooden trunk is right in back of the driver's seat, a pull down bed is hinged to the driver side wall, and two throne-like chairs are bolted to the floor surrounding a rough table. The entire interior is sheathed in wood, and that wood is covered with tapestry. At a glance, I spot "Lady and the Unicorn," "La Belle Dame Sans Merci," and there's a huge "Tree of Life." Alan sits in the throne facing the split windshield and gives me a quick thumbs up. He wraps his hands around the lion head carvings on the arms and immediately falls asleep, and for good reason. I climb into the passenger seat. The tall blonde kid taps me on the shoulder and then stares deeply into my eyes. His wide smile and thin lips match the rest of him perfectly. I can't help but grin back. He sticks out his hand.

"Tis a pleasure to meet thee. I am Robin of Locksley."

We shake. I introduce the sleeping Alan, and Robin bows his head towards Alan's wide mouth and heavy breathing. He then again stares deeply into my eyes.

"And what callest thou?"

It takes me a second or two to come back. Of course, I want to play. My mother taught fifth grade, and class never stopped at my house. Twenty-four/seven there was a metaphorical silver funnel in our ears, and she was filling it up with knowledge that she said we couldn't live without, and my late brother Jake was an athletic benevolent bean pole collection of Britannicas with arms and legs. You'd think that growing up in a genius family would have prepared me to meet Robin of Lockley, but no. You would have thought that I could have navigated the situation with ease. Hardly. The problem is that I haven't slept or eaten since Wednesday morning, and it is Saturday A.M.  I'm off my game. Robin has caught me flat footed. Alan, as he always does, comes to the surface briefly and saves the day with his brilliance.

"We art but wayfaring strang'rs, valorous Robin of Locksley. We art two m'rry men traveling through this w'rld below. I am hath called Alan-a-Dale, and this," Alan extends his arm theatrically towards me, laughing "And this sir, this gentle pilgrim, is valorous sire james of the hundr'd acre wood." And with that, Alan's head finds the padded corner of this high-back throne/chair and goes lights out.

"Yes. Well met," I say, grasping Robin's hand. "Indeed, I am Sir James."

Robin's smile goes over-wide. He throws back his head and laughs. He looks at me, nods, turns his face toward the ceiling and closes his eyes.

"Yes. Yes. Sing hey-ho, sing hey-ho into the green holly. Yes. Good Sir James of the Hundred Acre Wood and Alan-a-Dale. Merry Men, indeed. I've heard of thee, And I has't readeth of thy home since I wast three. A pleasure to meet thee."

I roll my driver side door shut, and we are off. Seconds later, the rain starts pounding down on the roof so hard, I can't hear what Robin is saying. That doesn't stop him, though. He just keeps on talking and gesticulating towards the road, always keeping one hand on the flat steering wheel. His big windshield wipers are working perfectly, and the road looks like a flickering old-time movie that I've seen a hundred times accompanied by a rainy drum solo. Focus, out of focus, focus, out of focus. and maybe it is the sound and rhythm of the rain, or maybe not eating and sleeping for a couple of days, or coming out of the cold into another century, but I fall into a different kind of understanding. I am entranced, mesmerized. I don't know what it is, but I felt like I have seen this road before. I felt like I know what Robin is going to say. I felt like I know what is going to happen.

Robin sees me nod off.

"If thee wanteth to nap liketh our cousin, Alan-a-Dale, I'll taketh a moment and base'r the pallet f'r thee?"

I don't know why I say no. It just comes out of my mouth like someone else is doing the talking. I would have loved to fall asleep. It is somewhere after 3:00 A.M. on Saturday. Wednesday morning the local police had picked us up, and we have spent that day, night, and the next two days in the hoosegow, a holding cell in the basement of the Moriah, NY courthouse. There has been an armed robbery in the area, and the robbers, apparently, were described as young scruffy long-hairs. We are questioned and re-questioned, interrogated actually, together and separately. I am told that Alan has confessed. I am told that if I confess and implicate Alan, I can go free. They feed us nothing, and interrogate us around the clock. The cell is empty, no bench, no bed, and between interrogations, Alan falls asleep on the cement floor. I pace the cell like a caged cat. Three days go by while we wait for the judge to appear, and by the time he does, the thieves have been rounded up. Friday night, the judge sends us packing and the cops drop us off at a pull-off just south of the town limits. They tell us that they'll be back in an hour, and if we are still there, they'll throw us in jail for vagrancy. When

Alan mentions that we have plenty of money, they think it's the funniest thing they've ever heard. Five minutes after they leave, we realize that they have helped themselves to the forty-six dollars we had between us.

They dumped us off around 11:00 Friday night, and, right on time, an hour later, we see headlights coming from town. We run for the bushes and huddle down low. It is them all right. One of them comes out with his flashlight and scans the woods. The other one calls him back. They are so close we can hear everything they say.

"God damn. We could have sold that fiddle. They're gone, but the night is still young," and they roar away, laughing, with their fins up.

We crawl out a good ten minutes later, and stand there, shivering in the 40 degree late-September night, without one car passing us until the smiley face. Unconsciously, I have been holding my fiddle case in my left hand the entire time. Now, it's at my feet, and my left hand is sore from holding it so tight in the cold.

"Wh're art thee two lonesome traveleth'rs bound on tis dark night?"

Inside the van's universe, with the wheel hum and the windshield wipers slapping time, I tell Robin how we had left Maine five days ago, and how everything had been going great for a while as we traversed the top of New Hampshire and Vermont, but New York was a different story. I tell him how we had lost my brother Jake to a drunk driver. From the darkness, Alan explains how the drunk driver was my father, and all three of us settle into the silence that follows. After a few minutes, I explain.

"I just couldn't look at that sorry bastard. Couldn't be there. I had to go."

"And what of thee, Alan-a-Dale?"

Alan says he couldn't resist a pilgrimage. "Ever read Chaucer? Anything can happen. Besides, I need to chaperone Sir James."

Robin thinks this is hysterical. He throws his head back, laughing, closes his eyes for a long second, and then looks back at the road. After he gets the van back in the right lane, he tells us that he and Geoffery are acquainted and says he's a British Literature major at Middlebury College. He says that he is going to drive all night, and in the morning jump into the arms of his "betroth'd," and then win the archery competition for the third year in a row, and play with his Merry Men, in celebration of the coming of fall.

"Wouldst thee liketh to cometh 'long?"

We both say that we are ready to celebrate anything.

"I might not but sayeth yond t'is one of mine own most wondrous fears yond the sh'riff of nottingham shall one day winneth, and yond gent, as a result, shall did lie the entire realm in cruelty and wasteth with the usurp'r, Prince John."

My wife stops me. "You can't be serious. Robin was completely Brit Medieval. He never broke character?"

I take a moment to explain."Yes," I tell her. "The guy was the story book character come back to life–far, far more convincing than Erroll Flynn was in the 1938 film. But something else was in play."

She takes a sip of her tea, shakes her head, and smiles. "What in the world are you talking about?"

I try to be patient. Poor girl. She grew up in a different world. She's not even sixty-one. I'm ten years her senior.

"What you have to understand is that it's 1971. Hippies are embedded into the very fabric of America. If you were young, you could go from being mildly eccentric to downright lunatic, and everybody would just wave you in. A guy like Robin of Lockley would be seated at the head of the table. That was a given, but we were only scratching the surface. The full and complete immersion is just up the road."

"Pray tell," she says. "I have basil to water."

I go on. I tell her we travel through the night. From Moriah, the scene of our incarceration, we pick up the Northway, and I'm surprised how the van can really move along, but then Robin takes RT 8, says it's a short cut, and we go from the middle of nowhere to the dark side of the moon. The rain comes on a little harder, and Robin slows down accordingly. We chug forward. Thirty-five miles an hour. When I glance back, in the instrument panel light, I can hear Alan-a-Dale breathing heavily, his face pushed into the padded corner of his throne. He's drooling. I'm feeling it, too, and then something shifts. I can't explain it. I get that feeling again, like something's about to happen. It's getting close to 5:30 A.M. We have passed Speculator, and are making our way south to pick up I90. Robin's in good form, telling me how he can't wait to see his betrothed at Locksley Manor, tells me "Th're is not fair'r in the landeth." Robin takes a moment to explain how "The w'rld is coming to locksley sir'r."

I don't know what the hell he's talking about, but we're warm and dry and in good company.

"We shall stand ho and feast at lockley sir'r f'r, and thee shall meeteth Lord and Lady Lockesley, mine own spaewife sist'r Isabela, and mine own twinsist'r, Hazel," which sounds just fine to me, especially the part about the feast.

My wife sips her tea, and carefully places her tea cup on the side table by her chair. She lays her hand on the handle of the watering can.

"How long was it since you ate and slept at this point?"

I shrug and sip my coffee

"Three days."

And believe me, I tell her, I'm excited about the possibility of an extended feast, but something has taken me over. I feel like I'm ready to be shot out of a cannon. I feel like I am the most awake I have ever been in my life. Seriously, I can feel the air on my hands. The hair on my arms is standing up. Goose pimples. Every raindrop on the windshield becomes an individual, the wheels of the route van are playing a symphony. Dawn is dawning, the light's coming up, I see a sign and we're about to go over the Mohawk River, and Robin's telling me how he's been practicing for the tournament, and how all of his Merry men in his band can't wait for the arrival of Richard the Lionhearted who is returning from his Crusade in the West. I roll down my window just a little, and can smell the woods, the water, I can smell honeysuckle and the coming dawn, and I feel it again. It is like someone's talking to me–just to me. Somebody's saying, "Get ready. Get ready. Here it comes, here it comes, here it comes, it's coming, it's coming," and then, right in mid-sentence, Robin's beard falls flat on his chest and he's out cold. We're careening right for the bridge abutment. We're going to smash into it, and then tumble down the fifty foot rocky embankment into the Mohawk River, but in a nanosecond my hand's on the wheel. There's not even a moment of panic. Not the blink of an eye. From the passenger seat I very easily steer us through the bridge and then make the hard right afterwards. But it's like there's a big hand squeezing my throat, and I can't say anything. Nothing's coming out. We're a couple of hundred yards past the bridge, I mean we're well down the road when Robin finally comes to the surface. When he wakes up, he stares at me a good three seconds before grabbing the wheel. Alan keeps on sleeping, breathing and drooling through his open mouth. I ask Robin if he's all right. He stares straight ahead.

"Valorous god. Thee has't did save us all. Thou art truly a most wondrous cousin."

For the next hour or so, Robin says nothing, but I'm shaking. I can barely stay in my seat. I have to wrap my arms around my chest, or I'm going to shake apart.

We get on I 90 for a while, and then around Syracuse, Robin exits, turns south on RT 34. Sun's up. We pass a sign for King Ferry, and Robin points to it like he's fencing with his arm.

"We art getting closeth, cousin. Lief, i shall beest in the arms of mine own loveth, and all because of thee."

I'm still shaking when we turn up a narrow beat-up stretch of road. He rolls down his window and takes a big, deep breath. The air smells like wildflower honey. There's a hand-painted arrow-shaped sign that reads "Michaelmas," and then another, and another.

"By the gods, home at lasteth."

Five minutes later we pull onto a dirt road with a beat-up blue mailbox. At the end of it all, right on the lake, my jaw drops. Alan has come to life.

"My god, who am I, where are we, and how did we get here?"

Good question, I think, but I didn't have an answer.

I'm thinking, maybe it's a movie set. We're in a movie. There's this funky tudor farmhouse and barn right on a lake, and the place is jumping with people–I'm guessing well over two hundred, and they're all in Medieval garb, I mean, there's not a pair of Levi's anywhere. There's a tall, thin, bearded man plowing a large garden plot with a gigantic black and white workhorse. He drops everything and starts jogging towards us.  People are crawling all over the place, setting up multi-colored tents, a crew is baking bread in an outdoor oven. There's a purple head scarfed young woman standing outside a purple tent under a banner that reads "Fortunes." When she sees me, she puts her hands on her waist and starts laughing, and then does that fencing-like pointing à la Uncle Sam thing that Robin does. Three young men are building a wooden stage. Two knights in armor are fighting with wooden swords. There are packs of hooligan children running amok in circles, and everybody looks like they brought their dog. When they see us, they all shout and descend on the van. The old man gets there first.

"Mine own son, welcometh home."

They embrace, and I sit there, everybody's face in the windows. If seeing smiles makes you rich, I'm a millionaire.

"And who is't art these brave pilgrims."

Robin silences the crowd around us.

"Prithee hark mine own family and cater-cousins."

The crowd goes silent, and I feel like I'm in the presence of King Henry at Agincourt. A young woman dressed in blue and white comes running into his arms. Yes, you guessed it: she's Maid Marion. Robin introduces Alan-a-Dale to the crowd, and then turns to me. I don't know why I'm still shaking, but I am. I'm giving myself a bear hug. My teeth are chattering. It's been almost two hours since we rolled through the bridge, and I can't get back. I just sit there with my dry mouth, trying to breathe slowly, but I can't.

Robin tells the story to a rapt, incredulous crowd, and then points at me like he's fencing.

"And this is the sir who is't hast did save our liveth."

The crowd busts into cheers. I am pulled out the van. A huge, bearded young man hoists me on his shoulders.

"This is the sir who is't did save robin hood. That gent shall beest mine own cousin f'rev'r."

My wife sips her tea, shaking her head.

"You can't be serious. You're paraded through the grounds. Maybe that's when you lost your marbles."

"I am. We are. Alan is a hero, too, but somewhere after the parade, things get fuzzy."

"How fuzzy?"

"I guess fuzzy as it gets. Real fuzzy. This is what I remember. We are ushered into the farmhouse by Robin's father and mother–I mean the Lord and Lady. They sit us down at a long thick table in their kitchen. Food appears in front of us. There's this bannock–a sweet bread, a mountain of scrambled eggs, stacks of pancakes, a pan of roasted roots, a pitcher of maple syrup. A young woman sits down next to me who looks exactly like Robin, and she's holding a screaming baby. It turns out that the screamer is Robin's young brother–the family trailer, and I mean, he's screaming. Everybody's talking at once. There's a huge Irish Wolfhound, Banquo, who puts his head on my shoulder, and then kisses my ear. I take a bite of bannock. The young woman introduces herself.

"I am robin's sist'r, hazel, and i shall nev'r f'rget thy valorous de'd. And this is mine own broth'r, arch'r."

Archer's mouth is one huge capital O.

She shakes my hand, but when she goes to shake Alan's hand I see it. Swear to god. I can see arrows come out of her eyes, going right into his. Swear to god, no joke, arrows come out of his eyes and go into hers. I'm in a Botticelli painting.

"T's thee," she says. She looks at Alan and says, "T's thee. I've been looking f'r thee, and h're thou art. Our life togeth'r shall starteth anon."

She passes Alan the screaming Archer.

"Brother, meet your uncle Alan-a-Dale."

And immediately, I mean immediately as in immediately upon contact, the screamer quiets and starts cooing. He reaches up and touches Alan's smiling face.

"Th're, moth'r and fath'r. Right th're. Thee can seeth yond i am not wrong."

The Lord and Lady smile, Robin shouts out "Hurray," I try to chew the bannock, but I can't. I am so, so tired. Shivering. The mouthful falls onto my plate. I stand up, like I'm looking for something, I know something's there, as in I've seen it before, and then I find it. Immediately to my right, there's a dog bed stuffed into the corner by the wood stove. I stumble over and curl into the rich earthy smell. And then nothing.

My wife stares at me. Perfectly still.

"What do you mean, 'nothing.'"

"Nothing as in nothing. When I wake up, it's the next day–close to noon. I mean nothing as in over twenty-four hours of nothing but the dog bed, the wolf hound that's sleeping next to me and my violin. Everybody is saying "Thank you" and "goodbye." I'm completely lost: moments ago I had just said "hello." I stand up and everyone cheers. Robin stands and waves me into a seat at the table.

"Our hero returns from the Underground."

And of course, everything has changed. He pats me on the back and slides a fresh piece bannock at me. Everybody's laughing. Everyone's in regular clothes speaking English.

My wife shakes her head.

"You're not making any sense again, which, you have to admit, is how my life with you has unfolded."

You'd think I'd get irritated at the comment, but I don't. All my life people have looked at me like I'm one giant green bird. I'm used to it. I just go on.

"When I wake up, I'm sleeping with the dog and my fiddle case, only to discover that we are guests at the Smith family's annual Michaelmas party–the Elizabethan celebration of the beginning of autumn. While I'm wolfing down roasted roots, Robin's father, Mason, tells me that he and his wife Hallie have been celebrating Michaelmas, the September 29th holiday, ever since they began teaching Medieval and Renaissance studies at Cornell over twenty years ago.

"And now, with the younger generation, it has gotten completely out of hand. The way it started was that all participants, for twenty-four hours on September 29, had to converse in Elizabethan English, and eat some roast goose, stuffed with onion and sage dressing, honoring Elizabeth I.  At one time, it was a linguistic immersion, and now there's meade, ale, and wine, and my son's rock band, The Merry Men. We have Robin, of course, on drums."

Mason starts identifying the players with the same fencing-like full arm extension. I immediately wonder if it is learned or a genetic tendency. Nature or nurture?

Mason keeps pointing.

"There's Will Scarlet on guitar, Little John on bass."

I recognize Little John immediately. He's the huge guy who carried me on his shoulders. Mason continues.

"And the young man with the black beard is King Richard the Lion-hearted, lead vocalist of The Merry Men, who has traveled clear across the country from Evergreen College to celebrate the archangels, the coming of fall, and the English victory over the Spanish Armada.. All of them need their heads examined. When did you gents finally quit last night?"

"At which hour the first cock didst crow," answers the short blonde haired boy, the one Mason just identified as lead guitarist Will Scarlet, and the place blows up laughing.

An hour later, we parade back to the van and load it with provisions. It's Sunday afternoon, and Robin needs to be on board for Monday classes at Middlebury College. Will, Little John, and Richard–The Lion-hearted are taking apart the bandstand, and I'm walking around like I'm in a dream. Right before blast-off, the young woman with the purple headscarf calls me over to the purple tent.

"Thee th're. Sir James of the hundr'd ac'd wood. Cometh h're."

She introduces herself as Robin's older sister, Isabela.

"I haven't had a chance to say hello. You slept through the whole thing. Our tradition is that everyone's fortune is told so that they can easily glide into the new season. I've told everyone's fortune but yours."

Her eyes don't leave my face when she's talking. I'm right in the middle of bright green headlights, and her purple scarf is the exact same color as the tent, and the two together are playing with my depth perception.

"You told Alan's, too?"

She starts laughing and points inside the tent. Her hands move like humming-birds. When they move, the silver bracelets on her wrists make music, and the small stars on her dark blue cape twinkle.

"I've told everyone's fortune. Everyone but yours. Take off your shoes, and have a seat."

I do. I walk in.

I sit in a high back chair. There is a low table covered with a red velvet cloth, and right on top is a white crystal ball. When she closes the tent flap, the place goes jet black, and then slowly the yellow stars on the blue rug at my feet start to glow. The shaking that I thought I had said good-bye to comes back again, and I wrap my arms around my chest. I can't see her, but I feel her pass me in the black. A moment later, there is enough light to see her opposite me. She lays both hands on the crystal ball and closes her eyes.

"Alloweth's seeth what the future holds f'r this brave knight."

A long minute later, the ball starts a low glow.

"Spirits, what is the f'rtune of this brave pilgrim bef're me? Speaketh to me, and i shall deliv'r thy message."

The low glow in the ball fades until I can no longer see Isabela, and that was OK with me. The last thing I want anyone to see is my shaking. I tighten the grip around my chest, but it just gets worse. I can't breathe, I can't breathe, I can't breathe, and then the ball becomes a bright white under her hands, illuminating the entire tent. Isabella starts giggling, and then looks up into my face.

"There is someone on the other side who needs to speak with you. Is there someone in your life who has recently passed?"

She bursts out in full laughter again, and shakes her head. Immediately, my shaking stops.

"He wants to know if you enjoyed the trip through the bridge? He says it was everything he could do to keep you awake."

"Jake," I tell her. "It's my brother Jake. He. . . ."

She talks through me.

"He says that if you're going to carry around that violin so much, you're going to have to learn how to play it in tune."

She bursts out laughing again, the ball grows brighter under her hands, and I don't realize I'm crying until she looks like she's underwater. In her hands, the ball looks like it's floating above the table.

"Whoops, he's serious now."

Her smile fades, and she nods her head.

"He says you need to go back and play some cello, violin duets. Wait. He's even telling you what to play. You're supposed to play Bartok's Hungarian Folk Melodies. And he says not to worry: Dracula has received his walking papers. Who's Dracula?"

"My father."

Her smile fades a little more.

"He says you need to go back. He says you need to take care of Jacqueline du Pré. Good lord, the cellist?"

"No. That's our joke together. That's what we call our mother."

She lifts her eyes into mine. There is no escape. There's no place to hide.

"Jake says he has to go. He says everything's going to be OK. He says that he's OK. He's good, in fact. And he wants you to know that you're going to be good, too. Wait. He's quoting somebody: 'If a man does not keep pace with his companions, perhaps it is because he hears a different drummer. Let him step to the music which he hears, however measured or far away.'"

A second later the tent goes jet black. I feel her move past me. When the tent flap opens, I am blinded in the bright light. When I can finally see again, she's gone.

We drive back to Middlebury that afternoon, via I90 and the Northway. None of us wanted to see the Mohawk Bridge again. We spend the night on Robin's dorm room floor, and in the morning, he insists we drive the route van back to Maine. We do, and Alan takes the time to elaborate on everything I missed, which is, as I mentioned, just about everything. I receive great details on the spectacular music.

"All originals. Fabulous. They were truly merry men."

Alan says that there was a canoe-full of ice and drinks, roasted goose, turkeys, and chickens on spits, blackberry cobbler, five gallon buckets of garlic mashed potatoes, round loaves of clay oven garlic bread, channel catfish and salmon from Lake Cayuga, and his personal favorite, whiskey-glazed carrots. Robin beat the Sheriff of Nottingham, a Cornell chemistry professor, once again in the archery competition. But Alan can't stop talking about Hazel.

"That girl is an angel incarnate. I'm not exaggerating. Do you understand? I touched her hand. It felt like feathers."

That evening, when I walk into our Frenchy house, The Hurrying Angel, my mother is playing the cello. She has given my father the boot, and she's there waiting for me. She knew I was coming. She says, "Can't explain it." She has a plate on the table, lasagna warm in the oven, and she's working on one of the Bartok Hungarian Folk tunes, "Által mennék én a Tiszán ladikon." "Crossing the River."

"This is the one that first caught my ear for some reason."

I've been gone for seven days. She doesn't even say hello. She just says, "You won't believe this dissonance. Truly spectacular. The man was spectacular."

A week later, Robin and Hazel arrive to bring back the van. Alan asks her for her hand in marriage, and she accepts. I mean, they're both eighteen. They're kids. They get married. They undergrad at Cornell, med school at the Mayo Clinic, and work together all their lives.

My wife sits there, and for a moment. I feel like I'm in the interrogation room in the basement of the courthouse in Moriah, New York.

"So what are you crying about? They're having a rich life. They've self-actualized, and now they're floating through France. They're somewhere off the charts on the Maslowian pyramid."

I try to explain, but I know it's not coming through. I agree with her: there's a long list of things not to cry about: Alan and Hazel delivered over 12,000 babies, Robin married Maid Marion, and has been chair of the Center for Medieval and Renaissance Studies at Duke for the last thirty years. My mother and I played all of Bartok's Hungarian Folk tunes, and then, just a few years before she died, she found true love for the first time as a middle-ager with our organic farmer neighbor, Joey Kline. And then, I try to tell my wife about our own falling apart farm and how I'm going to hold her hand right to the end, but it comes out jumbled. I get all tangled up. I try to tell her how privileged I've been to be able to lead students to higher ground. I tell her for over thirty-five years, it's been a miracle: I've been–and getting paid for it–teaching verbal insurrection and new-age Bolshevik theater on three continents at small colleges that struggle at keeping themselves in the black.

"It's like, for thirty-five years, I've been on the Lewis and Clark expedition, except I've been Sacagawea."

Her shoulders drop. She slumps in her chair and sips the last of her tea.

"So why are you crying?"

I put my face in my hands and rub my eyes. For a moment, I can see her better.

"I just never had a chance to thank Jake for keeping me awake. There would be no Alan and Hazel, no Robin and Marion, no Merry Men, no twelve thousand babies, no Lewis and Clark, no Sacagawea, no you and me, no broken down farmhouse, hundred acre wood, and basil bed. We'd be three crosses on the side of the road by the Mohawk River."

And then she starts crying. It's her turn. She stands up with her watering can and makes her way across the kitchen floor, but she's not paying attention. She's tipping the can, and an endless line of water is bubbling out of the long curved snout and trailing her across the wide pine boards.

She stops at the door, looks back at what she's done, and then points her arm at me. Good god. There it is again. It looks like she is fencing Uncle Sam. And now I get it: it's a learned behavior: nothing genetic about it. Or maybe it's both?

"You, Sir James of the hundred acre wood, are as weird as they come, and when you're gone, I'm going to break the mold myself, smash it to smithereens."

I protest. I tell her she's got it all wrong. I tell her that over fifty years ago I received my marching orders. I pull up my T-shirt and mop up my tear-streaked face, and for a moment, I can see her clearly. She's standing at the doorway in her Wellies, holding the galvanized watering can. The sun's on her face, and she's smiling under a yellow halo. Light pours into the kitchen and for another nanosecond, she disappears into it, and when I blink, her image slowly collects, starting with the green boots, moving upward. She reappears above the door mat. Somehow, Botticelli has gotten into the room.

I look at all the water on the floor, and then manage to catch her eye. I point at her face, fencing-style. I'm sending arrows.

"Nope," I tell her. "Simply not true. Nothing weird about me. I'm just not keeping pace with my companions. All these years, I've been marching to a different drummer."

# Apache Tears

Sitting in the hip café where everything
tastes the same, Big Joe gets in my
face, gnaws over an alien apricot
scone and assures me, between
sips of his high-voltage bottomless
coffee, that ten years ago he could have
slit my throat, walked away, and never
thought another thing about it.

Dysfunctional home life, says Joe. Wake up
scared and hungry. Get beat. Peel a bloody
shirt off your back at night. Makes you mean.

      The screen door slams as we
nod at each other, full eye
contact–Joe, brown; me, blue.
      Outside a chubby yuppy woman walks by
pulling a smiling blonde kid and his three
foot Pooh bear in a Radio-Flyer. Skate
boards. Sun bright on the street.

      But it would have been nothing
personal, says Joe. It was before
I found out about my native blood. Half
breed. Half badger. Half
snapping turtle. Before I
found out how to love everybody.

He laughs too hard and too long. I
pay the bill, but before we leave, Joe gets
trembly, reaches deep into his pocket, pulls out
the small green stone

                  and lays it

in my hand.


      If you ever need me, says Joe, you
      hold this stone. You hold this
      stone and think of me. Hold
      this stone and talk to me. Tell
      me the words as they
      fall out of your heart.


That was five years ago, and I
haven't seen Joe since we moved
out west. Still talk to him–from time
to time. Got a couple advanced
psychology degrees. Good
father. Teaches. Lives and works
exclusively for the people.

# The Third Tenor

(for Spencer Victor Wright, 1923-2019)

"And once you've got clocks, you've got death and dead people, because time, as we know, runs on, and then it runs out, and dead people are situated outside of time, whereas living people are still immersed in it."
—Margaret Atwood

My fingers clamp tight on the handrail, and in the inky dark, my toes curl around the edge of the cold December wooden stairs. I'm descending one at a time. I'm counting. When I hit thirteen, I know I'm at the ocean bottom, feel the icy smooth tile right through my wool socks. I keep the light off, so I don't wake him, but my head's still in the previous night's conversation. We were trying to land a brand new Corsair on the dark pitching deck of the *Enterprise*, the Big E. Inside-of-a-horse dark. Pacific. Fourth year of the war. Our tail's filled with holes, sputtering, no gas. Deck lights flash on at the last moment, can't see. Down. Cockpit fills with choking acid-blue smoke. Can't see. Squeal. Two bad bounces, stomp, mouth full of red hot copper pennies, hard hack cough, twice, then the tail hooks the cable. Whiplash. Home.

Spence calls my name from the next room.

"Hey. I made a mess."

I turn on the light. He's right, no argument there, and he is sitting right next to it on the bed, a bright pair of red plaid pajama bottoms circling his ankles, head down, bent over, wrists on knees, like he has just been benched at the homecoming game. I look down at his hands, making sure they're not part of the problem.

"It's all right," I say. "I'll have you back on the surface in no time."

"You really think this is 'all right'. This is not 'all right.'"

He shakes his head from side to side, lifts his eyes, and then locks them with mine, like he did teaching and coaching kids for thirty-nine years at Proctor Prep. Deep breath, lets it out slow, eye to eye, like there's something I don't get about the War of the Roses, Lord Nelson's navy, Roger's Rangers, Depression-era macro-economics, Pythagorean Theorem, the infield fly rule.

"Look. I need my pants changed."

"I know," I say. "But first a little rub-a-dub."

He drops his head. He's back again on the bench and nods into his hands.

"You're right."

He says it like Henry Fonda in *Twelve Angry Men*. It would not have been a reach to watch him pound his fist on a table, and stare into the face of each juror. What is at stake here is truth. Revelation. Possibility. We have to give this thing some air. There's a statue of a blindfolded Roman goddess somewhere out there holding a scale and the double-edged sword of Justice.

"But it's not 'all right'. I was just sitting here. You know, Hitler must have been crazy thinking he could take over the world. Crazy. "

He accentuates the word and points his finger at me like someone's going to give him an argument.

"The Japanese, too. Admiral Isoroku Yamamoto toured Detroit. He saw the assembly lines. He saw what we could do. During the Japanese celebration of their great cowardly victory at Pearl Harbor, he said, 'I fear all we have done is to awaken a sleeping giant and fill him with a terrible resolve.' I was just sitting here thinking how crazy Hitler was, and it got too late. I ran out of time."

"Not a big deal," I say.

"You're drilling for oil?"

I shake my head "no" and say it again, much louder. He gets it this time, but now

I have full-eye contact, head cocked a little to the side. All his lights go on when it comes to microeconomics and enterprise. Nothing like a bull market. His face stretches to full smile. My chance.

"That damn Hitler, " I tell him. "Never did have a sense of boundaries. And here he is coming back to give us trouble. Nobody invited him to dinner. Did you? Not on my guest list."

He looks up and shakes his head "no."

"Don't get me laughing."

Fifteen minutes later, the boat's bailed out. It's a bright, bright sunshiny day.

"I feel better already," he says, pointing his finger at my face. "But I need my pants pulled up, my shirt needs to be tucked under my pants, and my sweater needs to be pulled down outside my pants. Otherwise, I get cold."

He says that last part in a boxer's punchy, left, right, left. I bite down hard for a second, and then let up. I know what's on the way. This is where we suffer through the three or four second international delay, that overseas long distance call with the built-in transmission hesitation that makes conversational rhythm next to impossible and exasperating. This is where Emily Post reaches out from her manicured tasteful tombstone and gives me a good bitch-slapping. My face is about to light up red. Right on time, he says the word in a terse, Noel Coward cymbal crash.

"Please."

I bite down hard again. Another good opportunity to keep my mouth shut.

"I know," I tell him. "Believe me. I know how to do this."

He looks up at the timber framed plaster ceiling, and then at the giant gilded framed oil painting of his great grandfather that we put over the fireplace for him when he moved in. His mouth spreads to a smile.

"We sang 'Home on the Range.' Did I ever tell you that we sang at the carrier variety show. We sounded like a barbershop quartet, except it was just Kirk, Chris, and me. There was no harmony. We just belted it out. All three of us were tenors."

His saggy cheeks go wide when he says the word 'tenors,' and for a moment, his eyes look like two fried eggs, except in his case, the yokes are royal blue. After

I pull down his green wool sweater, he lowers himself slowly, then comes in for a hard landing on the new sheets. One bad bounce. The springs on his hospital bed screech. I hook my hand around the top of his head so he doesn't whiplash and crack into the wall. Home.

"Is Luciano Pavarotti still alive?"

I swallow the question a couple of times. I'm on thin ice. I squeeze my own eyes hard shut for a second. I can see that giant tidal wave of "O Sole Mio" coming in my direction. Luciano's been dead for over ten years, but not in my house. Here, his big chubby arms spread out wide, while he rattles every window, bounces off every crystal glass and shiny wooden floorboard.

"Not sure," I tell him, and then I act like there's something interesting outside in the growing light.

He just stares back at me, almost smiling, then slowly reaches out to grab last week's Sunday Edition in the basket of his walker. He comes close to getting there. We continue our routine.

"How about those two Spanish guys? Are they still living? When Luciano died, they were never the same. Pavarotti was the best one, and they knew it. He was bigger than life, and everybody knew that, too. Those Spanish guys knew it, and they went on. You have to face it, and go on. What did Luciano die of?"

"Cancer," I tell him like it's a brand new headline, *New York Times* breaking news.

Spence receives the information with one stoical nod. He looks at me to continue.

"Cancer was definitely one of his problems. The fact that the cheese cake didn't last long around that man was another issue entirely."

He squints, then opens up his blue earth eyes wide, laughing. The cracked lips are just going with it. I reach over and hit them with a little lip balm. I'm thinking finger in the dike.

"Stop it. Don't get me laughing. But you're right. How much do you think he weighed?"

I put my fist to my lips, raise my gaze to the ceiling like there's a number up there somewhere written on the plaster with a bold, black sharpie. His huge blue eyes don't leave my face, just like they didn't yesterday, and the day before yesterday, and the day before that, or a couple of months ago when we googled-up the question of Luciano's weight and got an answer.

I finally nod like it's come to me. He leans forward, and his bent fingers roll a little. Ten years ago he could have made fists. Ten years ago, he could have swung a hammer.

I throw my hands out in the air for the hell of it, going for baseball umpire power.

"OK. I'm thinking, and this would be at the height of Pavarotti's poundage, I want to say 350."

He whistles soft and low, and then nods like it's a figure that goes with a hand-shake. It's the nod I've seen every day for the past three and a half years he's been with us. I bet it was the same nod he gave his wife sixty years ago when he informed her that he had just purchased their first broken house without her consent. I imagine the same nod when my wife, his elder daughter, managed to smash the rear window on his brand new green 1968 Ford Country Squire. He nodded plenty at his four kids. Thirty-nine prep school graduations. Thirty-nine football camps. One divorce. Over fifty years of sales nods for Christmas trees off his Christmas tree farm. He nodded as the chief surgeon tried to explain what to expect after a hip replacement, the on-set of rheumatoid arthritis, his hospital-ization and near death with encephalitis. He nodded to a couple assisted living roommates, and then nodded to my wife when she asked him to come down to our farm and set up shop in our living room. When he got here he nodded at the little black dog and the six-toed cat that slept with him. Angora wool blanket, bottomless ice cold orange juice. Ice cream every night. Nod, nod, nod.

He comes to the surface.

"I feel better already. Thank you. You know, you're the only one who can really do this. Everybody else needs a little work, but you could be an aide in a hospital. You're good at this. You and your wife could take in a bunch of old people and make a business out of it. Is your mortgage paid off?

He raises those eyes to mine. Now, they are shiny, blue planet earths underwater. The sore that never heals on the bridge of his nose is oozing pink fluid, and what's left of his flaming red hair is multiply cow licked. I think of an abandoned osprey's nest covered with snow.

"I've figured out how you can split up the house and get five more old people in here. You know, you have a lot of wasted space, and you could make some money. You could charge every single one of them twenty dollars a day."

He sits there with his jaw clenched, fingers tapping-out Morse code on his knee, and then repeats himself, slowly, elevates the volume, his elocution like one of his ancient British ancestors, or maybe he's coaching the debate team again, or trying to communicate with a non-English speaker while traveling through Spain with Elderhostel.

"Charge each one twenty dollars a day." Raised eyebrows.

I wring out a washcloth in fresh warm water and hand it to him.

"This is for the face and for the head. Everybody has one of them."

"Don't get me laughing."

He presses it deep into his eye sockets, smooches it from ear to ear, flattens out the hair, chuckling under the washcloth-on-the-face darkness. When he hands the cloth back to me, it's in trembling T'ai Chi.

"When the Corsairs arrived, we pushed the Wildcats off the deck into the ocean. No joke. Obsolete, they told us. Pieces of junk."

My face tightens and I close my eyes. Yes, I've attended the lecture, seen the movie, read the book. Without wanting to or trying to, I mouth the words as he speaks them. He sits erect.

"The Corsair could fly over 400 mph. The Japanese called them 'Whistling Death.'"

Such a great name, I think, which would be perfect for this story that we've all heard at least several times every morning, noon, night, and at a number of times in between for the last three and a half years. I do the math, and the numbers get big. However, today, the sun's not even up yet, and everybody is, once again, pushing their Wildcats off the deck.

We nod in unison like there's an understanding between us.

"I actually pushed my plane into the ocean. Felt like I was batting for the other team."

He laughs, then stares at the ceiling, furrowing his extra-wide forehead. When he relaxes, four red stripes linger on his bone-white English skin.

"The irony was that nobody knew how to fly a Corsair. Sure, they could go 400 mph, but nobody knew how to takeoff or land on a carrier. The first two guys to attempt a takeoff slammed into the drink. Never saw them again. I was the number three man, but I can't tell you how I took off, and I can't tell you how I landed, but when I did, I bit the hell out of my tongue. When the deck crew pulled me out of the cockpit, I tried to thank them, but blood went everywhere. They thought I had been shot. My Landing Signal Officer looked at me and started to wail. I tried to explain, I tried to say his name. I tried to say, 'Smitty, I'm OK,' but blood just went everywhere. Everybody screaming for the Corpsman. The Brits finally figured it out. They stiffened up the suspension. After that, you could land a Corsair on a floating match box."

Both of us go silent for a moment out of respect for the two young pilots, who I've come to know. Both were twenty years old. Chris Fastie was studying biology at the University of California at Berkeley. He collected seven types of edible Pacific seaweed and somehow talked the cook into throwing it into the rice. Chris would go on leave, and come back with five gallon buckets of rotting stuff. He kept water samples in a hundred small specimen jars under his bunk. Kirk Webster was a farm boy from the Upper Peninsula of Michigan. Kirk was studying architecture at Michigan State. He could open a beer bottle with his thumb. Once Kirk cracked open a walnut by making a muscle with his bicep and squeezing down with his forearm. Right after the war, Spence visited their families.

He comes back to the surface.

"Ever happen to you?"

"What's that?" I say, perennially slow on the up-take.

He sighs, puts his bottomless patient face on again, the prep school face that watched kids fail the final, drop the ball, freeze in the outfield, forget Romeo's soliloquy, lose the priceless first-edition borrowed Francis Parkman, trip in the diploma line.

"Did you ever shit the bed?"

I get lost in the question. Sometimes camaraderie can only go so far. There are clubs that no one wants to join.

"It's not good," he says. "When you do, you won't like it. And it could be that once you start doing it, you could do it again, and again, and again. People would stop coming over to see you. And then it's your fingerprint. That's what everyone's going to remember."

He looks down at his hands like he is reading from notes.

"Not necessarily," I say. "People do a lot of things just once and never do them again."

"You really think so?"

He lets out half a laugh and a sharp little rise in inflection, like I had just announced to the entire class that the Danube river rolls right through West Virginia, Lewis and Clark were political activist singer-songwriters from the thirties, Harriet Tubman invented the assembly line. He dials in his spreading almost-toothless smile, his undertow of eye rolling and Buster Keaton double takes. Fifty years ago, he probably would have thrown chalk and erasers. He might have made me sit in the trash basket. Certainly, I would have had to repeat the year.

He points a crooked finger at my face.

"You know, you're welcome to your opinion. But when you play hard and loose with the facts, I have a problem. One of these days, you're just going to have to face it."

His blue planet earths get a little watery, and he locks in a five second stare. I know where we're going.

"Chris's entire family was there when I stopped in. I salute Captain Grover B.H. Hall, disembark from the *Big E*, get in a cab, and twenty-five minutes later, I'm walking through their front door. Chris lived just north of San Diego. Beach town. He was one of eight kids. I could hear "Stompin' at the Savoy" and hollering from the street. All seven of them are there, his mother and father, waiting for me. Everybody's drinking. His fourteen year old brother, Davey, slumped in a rocking chair, had passed out with a bottle of beer in his hands. Everybody's laughing and doing the Lindy Hop in the kitchen, singing in the kitchen. Cheryl, his oldest sister, puts her arms around me and kisses me so long and hard I feel like I am blind drunk walking on the bottom of San Diego bay. Then she bites my chin.

He does his nod and looks down at the floor, then slowly shakes the osprey nest.

"I should have married that one. But no joke, everybody in stitches. Chris's mother waves me over to her. 'Spencer,' she's shouting over Benny Goodman and the screaming. 'Spencer, this is where we are now. It's all we got. Every single one of us is all cried out.' Then she lifts her hand in the air, turns it a couple of times, and shakes her head and shouts. 'There's nothing left in the spigot.' When she says the word spigot, everybody goes bent over double in laughter. Cheryl kisses me again on the way out, and I feel like my lungs are going to collapse. She says, 'You're just getting the appetizers, Spencer Wright.' She says, 'You come back to California, we'll cook up some chicken cacciatore. Dessert? Cherries Jubilee.' She winks at me when she says the word 'jubilee." That was December, 1945. I never went back to San Diego. Cheryl sent me a Christmas card every year for over twenty years—until she died. She died young. I should have married her."

He looks at me a little fried-egg eyed when he says the word "died."

He clears his throat like a baseball umpire, spits into a napkin, and returns it to the basket of his walker.

"Ever happen to you?"

"What's that," I ask him.

"Anybody ever bite you on the chin?"

I just shake my head. "You see this thing?" I draw a large ear to ear circle in the air with my forefinger, and then tap my cheek. "See, smooth as a puppy's belly. I don't have the kind of face anybody would want to bite on the chin."

Spence takes a slug of the eternal orange juice we leave on his night stand and starts choking.

"Don't get me laughing."

He coughs hard three times, and then spits again into his napkin.

"Kirk's mother, Lucille, was a different story. They had a farm out on the Upper Peninsula of Michigan, father died when Kirk was five, and Lucille brought him up solo. Made it all work. Kirk said they lived off road-kill venison, lake trout, and dandelion greens. I made it up there in the spring of '46. Ice was still on Lake Superior, cracking like rifle shots and groaning like a whale. We drank coffee that could have melted steel and stared out her huge kitchen window at all the ice. I went out and split her a couple of armloads of wood for her immense cream and green Kitchen Queen cook stove, filled her wood box right up, while the wind tried to tear my face off.

Spence leans back and rubs against the cushions we've rigged up on the wall side of his hospital bed. We've been putting up the bars on the room side. In the last month, he's rolled off his bed twice.

"Lucille reaches over and fills up my mug, and I have to say, that woman had Popeye arms. It looked like there was a hardball inside her bicep. No joke. Then, she makes me tell her about our singing group, and I tell her. We're dropping eggs for the Marines on Guadalcanal, and Kirk starts singing "Home on the Range". Chris and I start singing, too, and then, it becomes our fingerprint. Every sortie, we sing. We told our Aircraft Controller that we were demoralizing the enemy. And I tell Lucille how at the *Big E's* variety show, Captain Grover B.H. Hall introduced us as "The Three Tenors." Can you imagine? We were first.

Spence points his thumb at his chest, locks his eyes with mine and raises his snowy eyebrows. He gives it a good five significant beats before going on.

"I tell Lucille that Kirk just kept singing, six verses, the entire flight deck jammed tight with men while Chris and I hummed low in the background. Not a dry face in that crowd when we were done, and we had marines on board. A lot of marines. Tough boys. They went off louder than a bomb when we were finished. Lucille freezes in her chair, listening, turns right to stone."

He points his finger at my face again. High eyebrows, then lowers his head, speaking like there are other people in the room, but he only wants me to hear.

"Lucille jumps up and runs to her Baldwin upright, pounding out that song. She says, 'Spencer, won't you sing it with me. You do the tenor.' We belt it out, all right. She knew all the verses—six of them, and I do that humming thing in back of her until we get to the chorus again. When we finish, I glance out the window, and see it. Swear to god, it's big as a plane, sun glowing off that white head and tail. It's a bald eagle. I manage to point at it, and Lucille throws her face into her hands and yells 'Kirk. Spencer, it's Kirk. He's here.' She's yelling and waving. And we both rush out into the full freezing gale while that eagle circles the house and barn, again and again, breaking our ear drums, yelling right back at us. We are freezing, and then it starts snowing, hell of a squall, with the sun out, both of us trembling from the cold, and Lucille waving up at that bird, shouting, 'Kirk. It's Kirk. My boy's here.'

Spence lowers his head and nods to the floor. When he looks up, his eyes are shiny.

"When I leave, she thanks me. She says, 'Spencer, everything's going to be alright from now on.' She holds my hand and won't let go. When she walks me to my father's Plymouth Woody, she reaches up with her Popeye arms and grabs the collar of my mackinaw, pulls me right down to her. 'Thank you, Spencer. Thank you for bringing Kirk back home.'

"An hour later, there's a good six inches of snow on the road. I slip my chains on, and just chug right though that great northern forest night, not a track on the road, heat blasting a small clear circle on the windshield. I don't slip a wheel. I was a man inside a car inside of a snow dome all the way home to Vermont, the entire time, the wind trying to push me into the ditches."

A gust of wind comes up and rattles the windows and doors. We both look out like it's somebody we know, wanting to come in.

I think I could stuff the entire French retreat from Fort Carillon into the silence that follows that story. I try a paradigm shift. Sometimes it's the only game in town.

"Hey, meet you in the kitchen. How about ham, eggs, buttered rye toast, OJ, raspberry jam, do some meds, and The Three Tenors."

I annunciate "The Three Tenors" slowly with additional volume, very aware of the power I command. Spence grins wide. I grin back, and reach again for the Chap Stick, get a quick layer on before he knows it. He rolls his nonagenarian tongue across the strawberry flavor.

"You can get The Three Tenors? Really? No joke?" And then the grey cloud falls. He looks up at me with his 1945 face. Watery eyes. He's coming in for another landing.

"Toward the end, in early July, we flew leaflet sorties. The leaflets said, "Get the hell out, we're coming." We would fly over burning cities, dropping paper. Yokohama. Nagoya. Nobody's home. Nobody's shooting. Those people were done. We bombed the hell out of them, and they were done. We're getting ready to invade, and every plane is a decoy. Kirk, Chris, and I spot this airport surrounded by houses. I don't know what happened to us, but part of it all is that war is hell, yes, but war is also boring. I look at Kirk and he gives me the thumbs up. Chris wiggles his wings. The three of us land on that tarmac. Do you understand what I just said?"

I tell him I do, just like I told him yesterday, and the day before that, and the day before that. I'm getting it, but this is one story I don't mind on loop. He pulls a kleenex out of the box on his night stand and wipes his eyes. It flutters down to the floor at his feet.

"People come pouring out of the houses carrying bowls of rice. Kids. Grannies. Grandpas. They're all smiling, waving, offering us their bowls of rice. Like they know us. Like we're their boys. Everybody waving us in. Everybody smiling, laughing, pushing these small bowls of rice over their heads. An old granny keeps waving at me like she had seen me take my first breath. I wave back, and she starts crying. And then we all take off at once. The three of us. Spooked. It was just too much. People scattering, waving goodbye like it was the last thing they were going to do. We all take off. In unison. We were just kids trying to sneak into the movies. We think, 'What the hell?' We find out later the rice is a traditional peace offering. Those people were out there negotiating, giving away everything they had. It's 1945. A month later, we drop Little Boy, then Fat Man."

It's the same silence that goes with the story. His hands are on his knees. Head down. He's benched again.

I give it another shot.

"Meet you in the kitchen. How about ham, eggs, buttered rye toast, OJ, raspberry jam, do some meds, and The Three Tenors."

"Sure, but not too much. You people are always giving me too much. Never seen so much wasted food in all my life. During the Great Depression, we ate pigeon for supper. My mother went away for four days, and we ran out of food. Violet, the woman who took care of us, showed us how to catch a pigeon, and we ate it for supper. You could feed five more old people in this house with what you throw out, and end up paying off your mortgage."

"Isn't too much better than not enough?" Sometimes, I'll try anything.

He coughs out a chuckle, and then raises his face, lifts his hands off his knees and finds his walker.

He looks at me, blinks hard, and then flinches like he's seeing me for the first time. Two blue fried eggs. On the third try, he makes it to his feet, take off, and after a significant pause, starts his T'ai Chi rattle across the floor. The tennis balls on the walker's back legs don't muffle the sound much, shuffling feet, bang, and I imagine a big band drummer, the ghost of Gene Krupa in the room, light on the high hat cymbal, beating the tom toms. Every once in a while there's a ka-boom crash on the bass drum.

Spence pauses for a moment, straightens up in his clean green pajamas, irons out his round shoulders. I imagine his Air Medal along with his Distinguished Flying Cross pinned right above his heart. He turns slightly to his left like he's addressing a wedding party in his Navy formal blues—about to give the best man speech; or maybe he's wearing his varsity club blazer and red striped regimental tie, extolling a classroom full of graduating seniors; a memorial gathering for a fallen Navy flier, DKE fraternity brother; honored guest trustees at the annual Christmas faculty bash; maybe the football team, down ten at half-time. Or maybe that's how he stood on the flight deck of *The Big E* with Kirk and Chris, crooning out "Home on the Range".

This time he doesn't smile and he doesn't nod. He hacks out a cough. He hacks again, then speaks.

"I want to be clear with you people. I am not going into the kitchen because I am hungry. I am not hungry. However, I will go into the kitchen, eat, look at my mail, read the paper, and take my meds. But know this, and make no mistake: I am going into the kitchen for the music. I am going into the kitchen for The Three Tenors. Those guys can really sing, and every single one of them knows how to face it."

# The Blacksmith's Dog Story

Twice, outside of LaDuke's Bar, you kept some
son-of-a-bitch from stealing
my tools, and twice, after closing time, I
found you at attention in the driver's
seat, the door wide open, so black
you were part of the truck
until your teeth sank into a stray
hand. The word got around that the smith's
bitch'll take your leg off at the hip
and that was true.

If I could run like you, I'd run
a few years back until our
act was on the road again. We'd
drive home worn out, beat up—
or run the roads all night
cold beer on the dash.

As it is, I had to wrap you in a blanket
after some yahoo thought you were a black
deer. I planted you nose to the north
with enough food to keep you
until you got where you were going.

# Spring Breaks in the Northeast Kingdom

With the lunar dust of one
long winter in your ears,
you rouse your darling

out of her sleepy elliptical
orbit and propose a cruise
into town. She squeals

with delight, and soon
the two of you lost planets
are on the move–

reclining into osteopathically
designed seats, a little
smooth music on the stereo,

You light up a menthol, offer
one to your love, and inside
a warm cloud see that

the road's going straight
enough and there's no reason
why you can't pull your baby

close, and she, with an air
of persuasion, sees no reason
why you can't help her

out of her clothes, which
you do with extraordinary
alacrity, which she returns–

starting with your shoes, moving
north, leaving you wondering why
poor boy, why is it you've never

pushed your foot through
the pedal, and slip down
this long, rock hard road.

# underground

**adverb**

Not openly

# Chilling Out in the Lincoln Avenue Cemetery
### (After Passing the Oral Exam)

I can almost recall the blocked
and sized words, all pregnant
with meaning, flowing
from my mouth as if
I were breathing life into some
dead thing. Sure, for an instant

I was magnificent, a whale
of a guy, the grin
of a moose. But then the men
fell on me with knives and teeth
biting into some soft
under-belly that was everywhere.

Verbally carved and well beaten, I
was then somehow let live. They
were nice men, really–
the best. Apparently, it was just
something I'd said, and inside
salvos of avuncular

laughter, they decreed
I should be re-educated
by a school of stout-hearted
souls where no one ever wins
an argument. Well, tonight

I've enrolled. Look around
stone hearties. Here I am.

# Revelation Arrives in the Monday Night Poetry Class

Our lifeboat holds fourteen. We're at sea. By 7:20, Miranda has a frown
so profound it could drape past her knees. Patrick's dozing-off
in his black padded chair on wheels because whatever it is
that makes his heart shutter all night in the dorm, doesn't visit him
in class. Ursula's focused on disappearing a handful of Juju fish
—hopeful the corn syrup and red dye will get her to 8:15, when she
can disappear with her friends into the soft bottomless Millennium
American night.
    But by god, I
have a job to do. I say "Ladies and Gentlemen—and all
genders in between—was Emily Dickenson correct
when she said, "Hope is the thing with
feathers/ that perches in the soul…"?

Maddi chooses the bottom of a well silence that follows to open the door
to her secret concealed cat carrier, releasing seven week-old
Pippin the Kitten—who makes it her job to float across our table, levitating over
everyone's laptop, pulling up all faces, hands and eyes open, the entire
room humming Vivaldi, shooting stars, didgeridoo, silver bells of laughter.

Ceremonious Keegan rubs his face and shakes his head. "No Sir. No
Sir, Captain. Hope is the thing that purrs and has a long silky tail."

# Henry Randall White Makes Things Right
### (Through the Explanation
### of the Difference Between Story and Plot)


"Where is the story? The story's in the dark."
>                                        —Margaret Atwood


A Poem in a Play's Clothing


**The Players:**

**Henry**: a very old man in a red buffalo plaid hunting Mackinaw. He is very dirty and unkempt.

**Roadhog**: a man wearing a dog mask. He sits at Henry's feet.

**Shillelagh Lady:** dressed in bark, twigs, and dark feathers, she carries a mighty stick. She stands at stage left during the play and holds up signs that she, Henry, the audience, and the Collective Unconscious will shout out.

**Audience**: Before the performance, the Shillelagh Lady will instruct the audience to shout out the words and phrases on large poster boards that she'll hold up.

**Collective Unconsciousness**: During the play, dressed in black, these four players cavort and gambol in  t'ai chi fashion in the shadows  upstage. They join the audience and the Shillelagh Lady shouting out the words and phrases on the poster boards.


Shillelagh Lady: (Pounds her stick into the stage three times) It's 3:00 A.M., late summer. The song of crickets is as thick as the darkness. Upstage, we see the silhouettes of trees in front of a full moon. Off stage, we hear a truck slow down and stop. A truck door creaks open. Two beats later we hear it slam shut, and then the sound of footsteps in gravel. In the darkness, we hear someone (Henry) say, "Come along, now, lad." We hear knocking on a rattling screen door. After a few seconds, there's some more knocking. Somewhere in the third round of knocking, the porch light goes on.  In the porch light, facing the audience, we see an old man, Henry Randall White,  dressed in  khaki pants and a red buffalo plaid  jacket and hat. There's a huge discolored wet spot on his pants from the zipper downward. His hands and face are clearly dirty, and there's an ancient bedraggled black dog-man sitting on his feet.

Henry: I'm sorry to bother you again. No, I don't know what time it is. It's 3:00 A.M.?
Is that

late or early?
Do you remember us? I was the old man who knocked on your door asking to use your phone

—and your bathroom—and then later, I drowned
in the lake. I've been appearing in your dreams for the last twelve months. When you awake, you're all sweat and shaky, and it isn't right.

And this is my dog—Roadhog.
Do you remember him? Of course. He sat on my feet when
I spoke with you. He won't fight with your dog. He's my best friend. I know that's a cliché, but it's a true cliché.

I didn't know what a cliché was until my son, Jeffrey, explained it to me.

Jeffrey was going to be a writer. I'm a civil engineer. I worked on the Trans-America Pyramid in San Francisco, CA. And Holy Cow, have you ever seen that colossus? You see these furry ears? (Henry points to his ears.) What's between them can convert everything into foot-pounds.

I just wanted to say, a year ago when we knocked on your door, I didn't know it was 3:00 A.M.

I didn't know what day it was.

Both Roadhog and I get up early, and we didn't know that you didn't. We're up all night anyway. We have to pee. We're the same age. I'm 82.  Roadhog is 13, and he's eighty pounds, which, according to my veterinarian,  converts to 82 in people years.

We were lost.

We were trying to find our way back home. A year ago, we had been on the road all summer, running away, I guess. We had one of those America the Beautiful Senior park passes, but now we're dead–and it doesn't matter.

You don't understand? Don't worry: That's why we're here.

I can explain anything in terms of strength of materials. I drive a black Silverado with a cap on the back where we sleep.

What's that horrible smell? I should step back? I'm standing too close to your screen door?

I'm scaring you?

Do you have children? You do. I have a boy. My wife is named Betty, and she's dead. Do you think you can love someone who's dead? I do. My son Jeffrey played football. He was a wide receiver. He was—I can only spell it—S-L-A-I-N in Vietnam. He rebuilt a British racing green 1959 Austin Healey 3000. Have you ever seen one? Jeffrey was S-L-A-I-N, but the Healey is still in my barn. It's on blocks, wrapped in three tarps and filled with moth balls to discourage mice and red squirrels. It's waiting for Jeffrey. Jeffrey had the greatest hands. He could catch flies right out of the air. He had a football scholarship to Stanford

University. Jeffrey

was a Cardinal. The red bird? He visits me
from time to time. First, I hear his 'cheer, cheer, cheer, cheer, cheer' and then I look
up, and it's 'Why, hello, Son. Thanks for checking in on your dad and Roadhog.'


You're going to call the police?


I just wanted to call Julie. Remember? You didn't have her number. She's my home
share guest. She thought it would be better if we split up the house. She made sure
we have a big screen TV in the basement. I can hear what she says to her boyfriend
through the floor. She says

Roadhog is a dump dog, and I'm a dump
man. She says I should drive my dump truck to the dump and take a spot in the
landfill. Julie says we're two fifty-five gallon bags of garbage—those are the biggest
bags you can buy. She says she can smell us right through the linoleum. Julie's boyfriend stomps when we shout too loud for the Cardinals.


Julie says she's tired of reminding me to change my pants.


In my good-bye letter, I told her she was wrong. We're not bags of garbage. We're
recycling. I'm more like boxboard. Roadhog is colored glass. And I told her she
could press her face into dough if she ever wanted to make animal crackers.


I admit, that was a mean thing to say.


You don't have a phone?


A year ago, we had been on the road all summer catching
pike and catfish for supper.

But then they stopped biting.

When the fish don't bite, Roadhog and I eat either Purina Beef or Purina
Chicken Flavor—and wild apples. I much prefer the beef. It makes
a thick brown tasty gravy. The young woman from the Blue Seal feed store loaded
in two 44 pound bags.

My father was a doctor.
I went to the Pennsylvania Military College.  I was a good shot with my Springfield
30-06. Later, we were issued the M1 Garand. I served in the European Theatre.
France. We took the Ludendorff Bridge.  I crossed the Rhine. Into Germany.

My son Jeffrey was going to be a writer.

Once, he explained the difference between story and plot, and that's why we  came
back this evening. Jeffrey had just read E.M. Forster.

You don't understand? It's not evening? The police are on their way?

OK.  I better hurry. Here's my story:

One year ago, an old man shows up at your door at 3:00 A.M. with his intrepid four
legged best friend

(Shillelagh Lady raises her "Road Hog" sign, signaling the audience and Collective
Unconscious/Henry to shout out 'Roadhog' in unison.)

Roadhog.

The man asks to use your phone and your bathroom.

He says he's lost.


He asks you to dial Julie for him. You do not open your screen door.  You tell him
you don't have a phone or a bathroom.
                                    You tell him to try
your neighbor, Wayne, who has a big light over his barn. On his way to the big light,
the old man falls into the lake.

                                        He  drowns. His dog drowns, too. Wayne fishes both
of them out of the shallow water the next day. See, a story—it's just


                    one damn thing after another. The events


don't depend on each other. They are just some occurrences—that happened.
Jeffrey said it's like rain, but if a story is like rain


                        I don't get it.


But my son, Jeffrey, who played wide receiver for the Stanford Cardinals, liked
plots. Here's the plot:


        One year ago, a very old man knocks at your door at 3:00 A.M.


He identifies himself as Henry Randall White, asks to use your bathroom, and he
asks to use your phone to call someone named Julie, but there's trouble from the
get-go.


(Shillelagh Lady raises her sign that reads "Da, Da, Da," signaling the audience,
Henry,  and the Collective Unconscious to chant the three descending notes

along with her that are typical in Film Noir soundtracks to denote and accentuate suspense.)

There's a huge urine inspired

wet spot on the front of his khaki pants, and there's the unmistakable sharp odor of diarrhea in the air. You discover, during your conversation with him, that he's been eating Purina Dog Chow and wild apples for the past week. What's more

he can't remember

Julie's phone number, who, as details unfold, is also somewhat suspect. In addition, he has an ancient, filthy, fleabag, comic strip dog sitting on his feet.

It's 3:00 A.M.

You have kids, and you're going to protect them with your life. Besides, this man and dog will track a trail of brown through your house, so you lie. You say you don't have a phone or a bathroom.

And because you have neither phone nor bath-room, you suggest that the old man and the dog should go and try your neighbor, Wayne. And because this old man is so old and dumb, he believes you. He's so old and dumb that he nods his big stupid head and scarecrow white shock of hair in agreement and asks with great optimistic sincerity

"Where's Wayne? He has a bathroom?'

And you tell him to head towards the big light through the trees because Wayne has an all-night big light hanging on his barn, and you can see it from your house. But there's an additional problem:

(Shillelagh Lady again raises her Da, Da, Da, sign, signaling the audience and Collective Unconscious to chant those three descending notes with her that are typical in Film Noir soundtracks to denote suspense.)

the moon is full and going down. It's shining its big light

right through the same trees much brighter than the light hanging on Wayne's barn. And because he's old and bumbling and clearly and completely out-of-it, bent over sick to his stomach, completely stained and demented

Henry Randall White heads for the moon

and instead of arriving at Wayne's barn, Henry walks into the lake and the muddy bottom instantly pulls in his feet like a giant leg-hold trap. There's a sucking sound. And because his feet are trapped, Henry leans over and tries to pull themout with his cartoon hands and arms, but instead of freeing himself, Henry loses his bal-ance, and because he's old and bumbling—sick from eating Purina Dog Chow, and clearly has dementia
(Shillelagh Lady again raises her Da, Da, Da sign. She, the audience, Henry and the Collective Unconscious shout out the sound.)

Henry performs a header

into the dark, three foot water. He falls over, and he can't get up. Because he can't get up, he starts thrashing, fighting for the surface, gasping for breath. Henry shouts out

(Shillelagh Lady  raises her Roadhog sign, signaling the audience/Collective

Unconsciousness and Henry to shout with her in unison, "Roadhog.")

Roadhog.

And because Henry is Roadhog's best friend, the ancient dog transforms into

Canine Baryshnikov

launching himself into the lake right on top of Henry, pushing him down further into the mud that once again releases a giant sucking sound.

And because they are best friends, Roadhog grabs Henry's arm and starts pulling and gasping and pulling. He chomps down hard on the sleeve of Henry's red buffalo plaid jacket. He's pulling with his entire octogenarian canine heart, he's pulling with all his memory of fresh fish by the fire and the years they watched the Stanford Cardinals dominate on their big scene in the basement of Henry's house while Julie garbage mouthed them from the floor above.

Roadhog pulls
and pulls, but within three minutes

(Shillelagh Lady raises her Da, Da, Da sign, Audience and Collective Unconscious respond accordingly.

Henry Randall White has drowned.

But because he loves Henry above all things, Roadhog strains and steels himself against the water and against Henry's demise. He pulls until his ancient dog heart bursts wide open, and he lies lifeless, floating over Henry like a defunct canine buoy over a demented dead man mooring. You see

Jeffrey explained it to me.

He was going to be a writer, and I'm a civil engineer. Jeffrey told me 'if you need to use the word "because" to tell your tale, you've got yourself a plot. It's not

like rain.'

Do you get it? I'm still not sure I do. But Jeffrey didn't get me either. Our brains were oil and water, writer and engineer. I asked him once, 'Son, do you even know what a civil engineer is?'

He said "Sure Dad. That's an engineer who's courteous and polite. Kind."

But this plot isn't about me. No. Absolutely not.

(Shillelagh Lady raises her Da, Da, Da sign signaling audience/Collective Unconsciousness and Henry to perform the Film Noir chant in unison with her.)

This plot's about you. How so?

(Shillelagh Lady raises her "Let Me Explain" sign. She, the audience and Collective Unconscious, Henry respond with a shout out.

Let me explain.

Because you owned the house, you came to the door. And because you were working three jobs, you're exhausted. You're exhausted and you have children, and since you have children, you'll defend them with your life. And remember it was 3:00 in the morning

and you're making breakfast at 6:00 and waitressing at 7:00, book-keeping at Peck
Electric after the lunch rush,  then working the circulation desk at the library until
6:30, then you come home and make dinner, bath time, brush teeth,  bedtime, story
time, tuck-in, kisses, night-night, drink one Miller High Life, read about three
pages of *Pride and Prejudice*—and then your lights go out.

Earlier that day, you tried out one of your jokes with your colleague, Shirley: 'Shirley,
what do you call a Vermonter who works three jobs?' Shirley shook her head. 'Lazy.'
So look, when you ran
into us, you slammed your door, you doused the porch light, dammit. Under your
breath, you even said I was, 'No Mr. Darcy.' You fell instantly back asleep, but in
your dreams, you hear two giant splashes, someone calling out

(Shillelagh Lady pulls up her Roadhog sign,  signaling the audience/Collective
Unconsciousness/Henry to shout in unison with her)

Roadhog!

—and then silence. Cold sweat aches. Shiver. Shaky. Sometimes

you wake the children, shouting out in your sleep

(Shillelagh Lady raises her "I could have saved them," sign,  signaling the audience/
Collective Unconsciousness/Henry to shout out in unison along with her):

"I could have saved them."

Sometimes you wake the children, hold them close, hold their soft warm round cheeks in your hands.

"Remember," you say. "Always remember. Momma loves."

That's why we're here. We're going to make it right because this is a plot.

(Shillelagh Lady raises her "Let Me Explain" sign. The audience, the Collective, and Henry respond together with her):

Let me explain.

Roadhog and I were old: we were going to die of something anyway, and now we're dead. And being dead is good—it's like being alive, except  you're always zippy, you're never sick or hungry—and everybody gets along. If people actually knew how good it was, they'd be jumping in front of cars to get here. So now, we don't need to call Julie or soil your bathroom, we're not sick and we're not hungry. We came back because

(Shillelagh Lady raises her Da,Da,Da sign. Audience, Henry,  and the Collective are in unison with her):

Let me explain.

You did nothing wrong.

You needed to protect your children. We would have ruined every Turkish cotton towel and heirloom Oriental rug in the house, and afterwards the entire place would have smelled like doddering old man and diarrhea dog.  You needed to work those tables–add up the light switches, and pass out the books, kiss kids in clean pajamas goodnight.

Guess what I'm going to do now?  Oh, you have absolutely no f-ing idea?

I'm going to take these two hands of mine and reach into your dreams. No joke. I'm going in deep, and I'm pulling it all out—

I mean all of it

the black Silverado, Betty, ferret-faced garbage mouth Julie, the 44 pound bags of Purina, Wayne

the full moon

the splashes, somebody hollering something, I'm even taking away the red bird cardinal and his 'cheer, cheer cheer', the Transamerica Pyramid. Hundreds of foot-pounds, the 1959 Healey 3000, the entire Vietnam war and the 3,000,000 people who died,  the Stanford football team, Roadhog leaning against my legs,  our stomach-turning rich stench—even the sound of my voice—and you'll sleep like a newborn kitten, a little lamb, or puppy dog, or better yet, maybe you'll

(Shillelagh Lady raises her Da,Da,Da sign. The audience, Henry,  and the Collective respond in sync with her, voicing the three descending notes.)

sleep like the dead.

From here on out, it will be like this. Now. Press your forehead against mine. Oh. You're not going to open the door? It's all right.

We can do this right through the screen.

Watch me. Hard to accomplish at this angle, I know. There. Lean in. Foreheads touching? Yes?

It's working.

Oh, I'm taking it all back.  Got my unwanted memory eraser going. See, I have yours right here in my hands, it's wriggling like a fish,  I'm holding on tight and taking it away

for ever and ever, and now

I'm going to whistle-up my dog

or maybe I'll just give him a shout. What? Yes, you can pull away now. You're good as new.  You have my personal guarantee on the matter.  From  here on out, everything's going to be alright.

I'm taking my dog and going home.

Roadhog and I are walking back into the dark to grow some wings, and you will never

see us again.

(Roadhog gets up and slowly walks away into the dark upstage)

Where's that dog gone?

(Shillelagh Lady raises her Roadhog sign. The audience/Collective Unconscious/

Henry to shout in unison along with her.)


Roadhog!


(Shillelagh Lady (Pounds her stick into the stage three times)
The stage goes black—except for the light of the full moon. We hear footsteps in gravel. In the darkness, we hear Henry say, "Come along, now, lad." We watch the full moon slowly go down behind the silhouetted trees.

# underground

According to Joseph Campbell:
"The rules and limits are unknown in this place."

"Once well underground, you know exactly where you are.
Nothing can happen to you, and nothing can get at you. You're
entirely your own master…"

—Kenneth Graham

# My Furniture Has Wheels

*My Furniture Has Wheels* is an excavation of cinematic storytelling—love, hate, pain, regret, death, eccentric *modus operandi*, familial solidarity—and ultimately— defiance in the face of the inevitable. Unsettling, strange, light-hearted, and often moving, the production explores memory, a life, and how to live it, through a combination of documentary and experimental filmmaking.

Opening with the monologue of a family patriarch, *My Furniture Has Wheels* is presented by an inspired, eclectic cast that includes the family matriarch, two sons, seven grandchildren, a grandson's fiancé, a son's significant other, a great-grandchild in *utero*, and a son-in-law. During the unraveling, the film embraces a touch of German Expressionism, along with the hard truth that William Faulkner has been telling us for the last seventy years, "The past is never dead. It's not even past."

Here's the film:

vimeo.com/384384359

# For Pete's Sake

My dog guards the door. My cat's
extremely white. And although
conversation's at an all time

low, we have occasional, long
sobering talks. I trust them completely
to repeat nothing. My truck's

an immovable art object. My tree
represents faith or commitment,
and Holy mackerel, stands

quite ill. I stand, too, whenever
I can, behind my window behind
my door, watching my friends seriously

croquet on my lawn. I gave away
my mallet years ago because I
know what I want. For Pete's
sake, I even know what wants me.

# Spence and the Thousand Days: A Play In One Act

**The Players:**

**Spence**: Older than god. Center stage.

**Hallelujah Chorus**: A group of eleven men, women, and all genders
in between,  dressed in various forms of stylized white football uniforms. Some
wear helmets. Some are scantily clad. The chorus always speaks and stomps in
unison and is positioned stage left, clustered on a slightly elevated platform.  All
wear football cleats.

Dark Stage.

In the darkness, the Hallelujah Chorus begins to run in place, faster and faster,
football cleats pounding in rhythm on the dais. A bass drum is heard in the distance, accompanied by a far-off brass band playing one verse and chorus of the
Notre Dame Fight Song.

A referee's whistle blows. All cleats stop. Stage lights up

Hallelujah Chorus: (Shouting) Spence! (Now conversational) Spence is dozing, sitting on the edge of his bed with a longhaired grey cat asleep at his left hand. Yes, he
is. He sits round-backed, head down, wrists on his knees. A walker is centered in
front of him. He is mostly bald with tufts of white hair cow-licked on the edges.  A
strange and unexplainable blue glow appears on the ceiling over his head and ever
so slowly, begins to grow. Spence places his shaking hand gently on the cat, very
deliberately looks up at the ceiling, then straight on, smiling impishly, excited to
see an audience.

Spence: I went one and nine that first season.

Hallelujah Chorus: Yes, you did.

Spence: Over fudge and sherry, Lyle asked how would it feel if Jack Camp took over varsity, and I went down to J.V.  I looked both right in the eyes and said, 'My furniture has wheels.'

Hallelujah Chorus: (Accentuated head-bobbing. They stomp cleats twice.) That's right.

Spence:  Sure, I said it, and I'll say it again—I don't care who knows. Jack Camp loved titles. I'd sit back, look at him strut around in his brand new camel wool ski pants, and I'd laugh like there was no tomorrow.  He could be the King of New Hampshire for all of me.

Hallelujah Chorus: Spence freezes for an instant, knits his brows. (Chorus pounds cleats twice in unison)

Spence: We were quiet. When we got off the bus, we were quiet: there was no rah, rah, rah. There was no 'Send a volley of cheer on high.' But on the first play, we hit them hard.

Hallelujah Chorus: Spence throws a short punch into the air.

Spence: (Pointing his finger enthusiastically at audience) On the first play, we hit them with everything we had, and those bastards knew they were in for a game.

Hallelujah Chorus:  You hit those bastards hard. (One cleated stomp. All throw short punches in the air.)

Spence: Have I had my supper yet? Have you had your supper?  I didn't ask you what time it is. I asked you if I can get some milk

that's real in a glass with the World News. Oh hell, give me another

glass: I need some uplifting to drown my sorrows.  Not too much. For Christ's sake, you people.

Hallelujah Chorus: (Demonstratively shaking their heads) Those people always give me too much.

Spence: Please.

Hallelujah Chorus: Spence grimaces and shakes his head side to side in an exaggerated manner like there's just been a bad call at home plate.  He reaches down to the table beside his bed in Tai Chi fashion and ever so slowly cups both hands around a half-filled glass of milk covered with a ratty used Kleenex. Visibly shaking, he brings the glass towards his mouth, blows off the Kleenex, and lets it fall on his lap. He drinks, then looks up at the ceiling and begins to chew slightly. During pensive chewing, Spence starts to nod, then slowly puts the glass back on the table.

Spence: We were quiet.

Hallelujah Chorus: (Turning to each other with fingers to mouths) Shhhhhhhh!

Spence: Sure, I said it and I'll say it again, don't care who knows. Jack Camp loved titles. He could be the god damned Grand Prince of Portsmouth for all of me, strutting around in his red lamb's wool snow flake hat. I'd sit back look at him and laugh like there was no tomorrow.

Hallelujah Chorus: (One stomp of cleats in unison) Spence closes his eyes and starts giggling, nodding, bobbing his head in an equine fashion in complete and utter affirmation.

Spence: That's right. Willie couldn't see. He was blind drunk, inhaled most of the barbequed pulled pork special with apple pie alamode, puked it through his nose into the gutter outside the Park Diner, came back in and ordered the same damn thing in a glass of milk with the world news. The old waiter had cauliflower ears.

Hallelujah Chorus: Is that so? (All cock their heads to the side)

Spence: (Nodding) The old waiter had been a professional wrestler.

Hallelujah Chorus: Spence closes his eyes, raises his face towards the ceiling. He laughs, chokes, then speaks while coughing.

Spence: (Coughing and speaking) There were some guys from Boston. They were Boston Irish. Some of their names started with O.

Hallelujah Chorus: (Coughing and speaking) They were kind of crude.
(Two stomps in unison.)

Spence: I never had any trouble with any of them. There was an unspoken law.

Hallelujah Chorus: (wagging fingers at each other) No fisticuffs with teammates.

Spence: Oh hell, give me another glass: I need to drown my sorrows.  For Christ's sake, you people, (slowly and with great emphasis) not too much.

Hallelujah Chorus: Spence lowers his head, and then shakes it, with great deliberation, from side to side like he's just witnessed a bad call at home plate.

Spence:  When Mr. Wright caught Chris and me necking on the red leather couch, we were quiet. Mr. Wright told me I had to leave, don't come back, but on the way out I stopped in the kitchen and drank
a long tall glass of water, looked that bastard right in his little nasty Pug eyes.

Hallelujah Chorus: Yes, you did. You did.

Spence: (Laughing) Looked like a little ferret, that bastard.

Hallelujah Chorus: The blue glow has slowly expanded across more than half the ceiling. Spence raises his face to it once again, and stares wide eyed for a good three seconds.

Spence: (Wide eyed) We were quiet. I've told you this story.

Hallelujah Chorus: (Nodding emphatically and laughing, some put their faces in their hands, some put their hands over their ears.) Yes you have. Yes you have. You (All pointing at Spence) hit those nasty Pug-eyed ferret-faced Boston Irish bastards hard on the quiet couch with cauliflower ears. (One cleat stomp)

Spence: (Nodding) That's right. Willie couldn't see. He was drunk blind, gormandized the majority of the Farmer's Barbequed Chicken and Biscuit special, smashed potatoes with pecan pie alamode, up-chucked the entire extravaganza through his ears into the gutter outside the Park Diner, fell back into a professional wrestler and ordered the same naval bombardment is the world's most concentrated fire power. It's a frightening thing. I told June, 'You don't want to be on the receiving end.'

Hallelujah Chorus: (Wagging fingers back and forth and shaking their heads, suggestively) No you don't, June. No you don't.

Spence:  June said, 'I'm sitting right here on your lap and not
moving until you kiss me.  Please.' She sat there until after midnight. She sat there
in the snow.

Hallelujah Chorus: Yes she did. Yes she did. (Two stomps)

Spence: When Mr. Wright caught us necking on his monster red leather
couch, he told me he'd never hire me at the bank, but on the way
out I stopped in the kitchen, looked Mr. Ferret Face right in the eyes, said I needed
to invest in some chocolate ice cream with some chocolate sauce, cherry on top
with a long tall glass of water.

Hallelujah Chorus: (Shouting) Please.

Spence: I looked at his little nasty raccoon eyes. (Laughing and coughing) He
looked like a little nasty raccoon about to bite.

Hallelujah Chorus: Yes, he did. Yes, he did. (One stomp.)

Spence: I took my time. After twenty years, I told Lyle I would have
worked for nothing. Lyle adjusted
his red and blue Grenadier Guards tie and said, 'This news
is hurting my ears

                        a naval bombardment is the world's most concentrated fire
power. June said, 'I'm sitting right
here on your lap until you kiss me.' She sat there until after
midnight. She sat there in driving rain and snow singing 'Have I had supper? Have
you had your supper?' I told June, 'We
hit them as hard as we could.'

Hallelujah Chorus: (Gasping. Short of breath)  Spence tilts his peachy face upward. (One stomp.)

Spence: June, Honey. Listen, it's a terrible thing. You don't want to be on the receiving end.

Hallelujah Chorus: The blue glow has stretched over Spence like an umbrella. He exaggeratedly knits his brows, and speaks to someone over his head.

Spence: Ernest Sherman said it was too snowy to take the team on the road, told me to cancel the game.

Hallelujah Chorus: (Incredulous) What? Cancel the game?

Spence: Ernest Sherman asked me if I was crazy. He said I was putting young lives at risk for the sake of a game. He said cars and trucks were off the road all over New Hampshire. He asked me if I was going to enjoy speaking with parents in the hospital or maybe even the graveyard.

Hallelujah Chorus: (All put hands on hips) Are you crazy? (Two stomps)

Spence: I asked Lyle what I should do. Lyle said, 'It's your decision.'
(Points his finger at the audience)

Hallelujah Chorus: (Pointing their fingers) I have a message for you, Mr. Ernest Sherman.

Spence: (Laughing, pointing again at audience) I said 'Everybody on the bus. I don't give a damn if it's snowing in Buffalo.'

Hallelujah Chorus:  (Derisively, shaking heads) Ernest Sherman. (One stomp)

Spence: I don't give a damn what time it is. I asked you if I can have some milk that's real when Mr. Wright caught Chris and me necking on his red hydra monster leather couch, I was wearing my blue
tennis shoes, which he took issue with on my way out through
the kitchen I saw Mike Diaz vomit into his scotch whiskey
sour, smile, then drink it, a long tall glass on the rocks.

Hallelujah Chorus: (Shouting, shaking heads from side to side. All put hands over their ears) Please. (Two stomps)

Spence: For the love of god, I'll say it again. I don't give a damn if it's snowing out in Buffalo. Everybody get on the damn bus.  Ernest Sherman, I'll meet you in the graveyard.

Hallelujah Chorus: Quiet, June, Honey.

Spence: Have you ever noticed that when the guy's a real bastard . . .

Hallelujah Chorus: Spence looks up at the blue glow. It has completely covered the ceiling and is now raining down the walls.  Spence reaches over in Tai Chi fashion with his left hand, visibly shaking, and strokes the longhaired grey cat, smiles, and scans the room like a search light.

Spence: (Nodding emphatically) When the guy is a real bastard, his wife is always a good egg.

Hallelujah Chorus: Yes, she is. Yes, she is.

Spence: She's a good egg.

Hallelujah Chorus: Spence pauses, looks straight ahead, sets his face in a grimace, then grins impishly, his face exploding in laughter. He reaches out, grabs his walker, and on the third try, rises to his feet, coughing and laughing.

Spence: Lyle served us a rather nice port and hazel nut fudge. I complimented the drink. It was good stuff.

Hallelujah Chorus: For the love of god, let's have some of that good stuff. (All mime drinking)

Spence: Lyle adjusted his red and blue Grenadier Guards tie, then asked me how it would feel if His Excellency, the venerable Swami, Admiral of the Fleet, Mr. Big Ski Pants El Supremissimo, the Honorable Commodore, His Holiness Jack Camp took over varsity, and I dropped down to J.V. I planted my foot, laughed, then let them both have it. I told them, 'There's no tomorrow. For Christ's sake you people.'

Hallelujah Chorus: Very unsteady and in Tai Chi fashion, Spence lets go of the handles of his walker, extends his arms, turning his palms upward, hands shaking, looking like he's charged with electricity.

A referee's whistle sounds off stage. In the distance, the Penn State Fight Song begins to play. Spence waves wildly to the crowd, pointing and nodding to imagined specific individuals like Hillary Clinton did on the campaign trail. During this time, The Hallelujah Chorus creates a sustained rumble of staccato stomping. While staccato stomping, they wave, laugh, and point wildly to the crowd in complete and utter mockery. The Penn State band sings a verse *a cappella*. A referee's whistle sounds off stage.

Hallelujah Chorus and Spence: (Shouting together) My furniture has wheels.

Stage falls into darkness and silence for three beats.

Hallelujah Chorus: (In darkness. Shouting, then descending in volume until the last is a whisper with *ritardando*)

Fight, fight, fight.
Fight, fight, fight.
Fight, fight, fight.
Fight, fight, fight.

<h1 style="text-align:center">Last Letter of Encouragement</h1>
From Good Grandfather Lunguaard)

Brownie the dog and I walk
around the block and around

the block, and around
here everything is snow

rain and old bones
keep going and going Jimmy

marry yourself a rosy
cheeked farm girl with big

knocks we all can be proud
of a few bambinos too

at dinner table spilling
milk while you get

success in business everybody
will wave to you in town

not like you was as a boy
I remember you so sulky

Sometimes I was speaking
to Ralphy remember him smart

old gun he is dying of something
I forget you turn around

and you turn around and you
say you're happy with no

sweetie and little boy
don't forget me sometime

but bastard you promised
and never showed like

last fall remember to tell
the truth I told you

keep your nose clean sincerely
and regards with love as ever

work good and bye.

# underground

: produced or published outside the establishment especially by the avant-garde. Those seeking to explore alternative forms of lifestyle.

"The underground is dark and suffocating. But there is gold down there."

—Carl Jung

# On the Brink of Leaving Holiday Town

House sit. Make sure the heat's down low. Trash
day. Feed the cat. Water the plants. Eat someone
else's porridge out of some else's bowl. Sit
all morning in their favorite chair. Stack some

wood, or dangle all night from the hands of the town
hall clock crying: Mercy. Crying: Help–Murder
        –Thief, and not even get

the bark out of a dog on a clear night–like
this one–with insomniac me and my lucky
shoes circumambulating the preferred
residential sections of a town
famous for its fireworks, Easter bunnies, jack-
o-lantern parade. Circumambulate

        all night, and in the morning, peach
scones at the bakery, coffee, twelve
o'clock whistle, glory hallelujah ringing
out of the church bell tower at  5:00, three
screaming blonde kids getting pulled in a purple
sled on the snowy sidewalk past the yelping
grey hounddog by a woman young enough to get
pulled herself. Cold, and head

down in the cold. Slide past the commemorative
civil war cannon to the dark-wood civil war
library, where I will spend the evening miraculously

reading wounded leather-bound classics under the inadequate
yellow light, until it's time to watch the local

angels pulling the moon across the sky on a long
black wire–until it's time for my drifter's
heart to jump out of its chest and fly–
and for me to run wildman after it
–howling rag-tag down the road.

## Paging Long Lost John

He lived on some high ground back in the deep
swamp–in the middle of a maple grove, a small
creek running close to his cabin. Screened-in
porch. One rocker.
                 Hunted. Fished. Kept
chickens. Paddled out every Saturday to go
dancing. Even bought a red cowboy shirt and lizard
skin dancing shoes.
                 Loved women, kids, and dogs–and got
seriously loved back. Heard he had the gentlest
callused hands
                 for a big man. Hired out. Sold
pelts. Picked apples. Sugared. And walked
around, light on his feet, talking
to himself–
                 generally laughing. Disappeared
one winter–everybody thinking he fell
through the ice–his place nailed
tight together until the wind started to work
the doors and windows–until the wind got
inside and wore out the rugs. Flooded
the next spring.
                 Even thought I saw
his rocker floating under
the bridge in town, along with various
other junk, debris–on its
way to the lake no doubt. Still
wouldn't mind seeing him some

Saturday night–
                    all slicked
up in the breeze, hair
toniced, popeyed, endless
chatter-giggles, and a little
shiny around the edges like he knows
something–or like he might even
tell us what there is to know
under all that slack water and scrub woods.

So in the meantime, there's nothing
else to do, so I'm just putting my
hands together and shouting
out the windows into the black
night. I'm just
sitting here by the windows
shouting out into the night, "Talk
to me John. Are you
there? Are you there?"

# Getting Back to Dash

Thousands of miles, boy–and each one has
something to say. Roll. Tire song–in coded
form, of course–always trying to tell you
everything, like me, I suppose. I'm

standing on the edge of this tired road trying
to tell you everything so puzzling
sad and true, it could be right out of the great
Book of Revelations. Take the girl

you loved, for example, and brace yourself. Now
she loves you back. Now she loves you back so
hard you've become arms and legs again, big
wet kisses and drops of cum. She loves you back so
hard, she wakes up in the middle of the thick
black night laughing, stretches out her soft
white hands like you're going to fall
into her arms. And when she imagines you've
fallen into her arms, she'll fall back
asleep, and all the time so mysteriously
sad, insane–systematically creating

broken toys all over the dirt yard, grass stained
pants on the line, unforgettable
spaghetti accidents, and you coming home
–every afternoon–wide grin, cartoon
lunch box, stupid hat–in imperturbable
jubilation. Dash, this girl falls asleep

systematically re-discovering that she's

in love and you're dead, or that she's about
to break in half and you're dead, or that she's
held someone who reminds her so much of you, she can
almost make you out: blue/white teeth, brown beard, Italian
nose, big kind eyes–maybe the guy walking

on the other side of the street with his
hands in his pockets, short jacket, guitar, funny
shoes–saying something to himself, as if there's
something you left unsaid, perhaps a little
wheel music inside every inner revolution along
thousand of miles of tired road.  I

don't know, so I listen, or just stand on the edge of this
highway with my hands in my pockets, shouting out
all the news, every name I know. I am shouting on the edge
of this world in all directions, as if you can hear me, as if
you want to hear, faithfully anticipating a Miracle
of Revelation will rise, roll on, and let you shout back.

## The Bilingual Sky of Madrid: An Epithalamion

"On one end there was who you were before you went
underground, and on the other end a new person steps out
into the light."

—Coleson Whitehead

The bride looks like Grace Kelly from *High Society*. The bride's
sister, who will officiate the ceremony in three days at El Palacio
Juan Carlos III, looks like Grace Kelly from *To Catch a Thief.* I do
an entire 180° inspection of the Hotel's Villa de la Reina pent-terrace
restaurant that overlooks the Parque del Retiro–the same 125 hectare
park and royal palace Napoleon  destroyed in 1808. My search
is fruitless: Without doubt, nobody on the terrace looks like Cary Grant.


The rooftop Spanish breeze comes on full in our faces, and from
my myopic stronghold at the eastern end of the Romanesque
ten meter Spanish table, the bride's mother—my wife—looks like
a cross between Anne of Green Gables and Shirley Temple from the 1934
classic *Bright Eyes.*
   She is laughing and hand translating with the groom's
father, who's emphatic about the Brits  returning Gibraltar. He looks like King
Ferdinand II of Aragon. When he stands for a toast, the medals on his jacket
glitter in the setting sun.
    "To all my family, friends—and new family—who have
traveled from thirty-seven different countries from
around the world to celebrate with us."


When I raise my glass of water, all Spanish glasses go down. The groom's
mother, who looks like the Queen Isabella who signed-off on the Columbus

expedition, explains: "In Spain, to toast with water is very bad luck."

I lean back into my throne-like wicker chair. At 7:00 P.M., in the ancient
capital in the land of bears, built on Arabian stones, the blood orange sun
freezes directly over Pico Peñalara in the west. The parched brown
Madrileño hills turn pink. The city goes Picasso. The groom's elder sister, who
looks like Princess Catherine of Aragon, speaks:

"There is no other like the sky of Madrid."

I try out my thoughtful Spanish face: raise my eyebrows, push out my chin, shrug
my shoulders, tilt my head, then agree, privately wondering if the forest
fires of Portugal have anything to do with it.
Three Spanish aunts
arrive, having escaped from a Joaquín Sorolla beach painting. They lead
a promenade of humanity. I count the complicated house: there are
fourteen Spanish cousins, the Peruvian ambassador to Bretaña, the bride's
father and angelic second family, a red-haired American uncle, a red-haired
American aunt plus significant, six fair American cousins, two Kenyan second
cousins plus daughter, the step-mother's CIA step-uncle brother, the bride's
step-grandparents from Colorado, MIT MBA classmates from Australia, two
neighborly Bostonian dog walking compañeros, and the officiate's
husband, who looks like Jimmy Steward from *It's a Wonderful Life*. He's
holding the wedding's celebrated 2.5 year-old suspendered and bow-tied
groomsman, whose face is lathered in extra-thick Spanish red tomato
spaghetti sauce.
The groomsman raises his head, smiles, shows me the tiny red
car in his left hand, then face-plants asleep into Jimmy Stewart's immaculate
white shirt. The other faces on both sides of the union suddenly disappear
into a whirlpool of Spanish kissing.

I take the moment to familiarize
myself with the terrace pool rules that are posted in international stick
figures against the thick green glass: I think suits are not optional. The groom's younger
sister, who looks like Audrey Hepburn from *Breakfast at Tiffany's*
corroborates:

"In Spain, we find that German tourists in particular need
specific instructions."

Additionally, dogs are not allowed, not even diminutive
adorable curly-haired dogs of Spanish descent. And there will be no
diving into the 39" deep water. What's more, guest swimmers are forbidden
to climb over the pool's outer rampart wall and fall eight stories to their
deaths on the beautiful, mosaic river stone sidewalk  below.


The sun disappears behind the Sierra de Guadarramas. The terrace
vibrates in the crimson light. I decide not to go swimming. I'm staying
put. If I had a flag, I'd plant it right here next to the grilled octopus
and sardines on toast.

The groom taps his wine glass, and in the impressionistic
Academy Award-winning  Spanish light, he looks like Cary Grant. Grace Kelly embraces
 Grace Kelly.  The tomato-clad niño lifts his head, only to fall deeper into
Jimmy Stewart's white cloud shoulder. The bride closes her eyes. She speaks:


"Everyone. All of you. Todo el mundo. Everyone I love in the world. Todos
lo que amo  en el mundo. Is at this table. Están justo aquí en esta mesa."


She nods. Someone claps to break the silence. Someone shouts "Salud." Isabella
of Aragon presses  a full flute of cava into my left hand.  I raise it, high
into the dry evening air with the others. We stand. And now, all of us, blinking
together in rosy Spanish light, we have all the luck in the world.

# Man School, First Day

> "It took me a long time to figure out that the youngest in a
> family of dragons  is still a dragon from the point of view of
> those who find dragons alarming."
> —Margaret Atwood


I was just a little longer than the gun, and just about
as skinny. I held

      the stock as tight as I could, but that sweet
Browning twenty gauge over and under took my shoulder clean
off anyway.

      The red and white Campbell›s soup can, the target, hung
in the pale blue sky like it was swinging from a wire. The can
froze up there, and then started slowly spinning.

      It froze up there
for a good while, and then nosedived, clanked and bounced
on the gravel road.

      For a few seconds, I was rising off the ground. I could
hear the ocean and church bells. I could taste dirt. The honeysuckle
on the banks was emerald green and covered in white blossoms, bright
orange tiger lilies high above it,  yellow roses climbing across
freshly painted white picket fence, honey bees humming over
new mowed lawn.

      When I brought my face away from the stock, the smell
of Hoppe's gun oil stayed with me

      penetrating into my
hands, my cheeks.

      I could taste it, too,  and I could feel every
pebble of checkering on the walnut stock's pistol grip and forearm.

I liked the high tide baritone laughter. I liked the rough slap on my back.

I can't see your face in the sunlight, and then there it is. Big, chiseled
jaw. Smiling. You could have been a double for Teddy Roosevelt in Ray Ban
aviators. Hunter green western shirt, turquoise bolo tie, wide brim brown Stetson.

"Oh yes, Sir. Yes Sir. You're a shooter. I can spot a natural. Guaranteed."

I nodded with an open mouth grin. A black and white setter dog
strolled over and leaned against my bare legs, and then sat down
right on the toes of my sneakers. The man's hands eased the Browning
off my shoulder.
There was a flash of bright August sun, the rough
bark on the sycamore tree. When I reached down to pet
the dog, my hands and arms shook in the white hotlight.

# In the Middle of the Tall Night
### (On the Purple Hydrangea-covered Rainy Island  in the Middle of the
### Volcanic Rock Salt Sea, Laudelino António Rodriguis Gomes Wakes and
### Speaks with the Ocean)


for Marc Estrin

Life here. Life there. I tell myself, life is endless

considerations,  so many people I want to be. I am

hundreds of strung together big moons and suns. Look

here, there is an entire Gothic city floating between

my ears. Every day,  I'm eating Neapolitan ice cream and raspberry

cake at my own birthday party, and every night I pull

a bottomless dark blanket filled with stars over my exasperated

marble head, but Oceano, he appears.


"You, Laudelino. Wake up. You can sleep when you're

dead. There is no time to lose. Bravura, Laude. Be

someone brave. Time to choose your way."


So I wake up. OK. I wake up. In my dreams I was the fog

on the window,  I was a sailor man, my splendid

red face in the wind. I held the wheel of a great

Baltimore Clipper, and then a blacksmith's

hammer, a shipwright's plane, and then I was holding

the hands of little children,  an enormous red heart

thumping out of my chest, rolling down the road. I wore a white

coat and stethoscope. I wore a leather apron. I stood

tall, white wigged,  in front of a supreme judge and jury.  Fine bay

horses cantered with black and white shepherd dogs circling
long fleeced sheep. I was a wind-blown blue
violinist perched on a rooftop, playing for an angel on my
shoulder–and a thousand smiling faces and their punctuating
applause. I slept inside a huge, spinning crystal green globe.

So yes. OK. I wake and walk down to the fishing boat
harbor, but I carry it all inside my ragged cyclopean head and watch
ten waves taller than a house roll in. Ten waves, a north
to south breeze, a light in somebody's fourth
story window. Oceano, he speaks:

"Laudolino, every night the sea swallows the moon, every
day the sea spits out the sun, and one's heart leaks out a little life."

So I say to him:

"I have been saying the *Fátima* prayer, and I even
conceptually see this world like a big
wheel spinning round and round–and that's
right, I think, and right now, I have
a birthday party going on between my ears."

Oceano lets his waves roar. His words follow.

"One can let a hundred gales blow in one's
face, and in a moment, one is old, and in a moment
one will die, and in a moment, the stars will roll
out of their dark blanket and light one's way
along this foggy river."

But the stars do not light my way tonight, quite frankly. Tonight
the stars let me walk home in blackness–so black I can
barely feel my own small flutter heart that God has so
graciously given me. Yes. There are many lives to lead.  I
look up. I shrug my shoulders, lift my open palms.

"*Se Deus quiser.* If this is God's will."

In the silence that follows,  Oceano hums and lays his cool
fingers on my shoulder.  I cover my furry
ears with my hands. I cover my fried egg eyes.  How
can I hide? He is taller than ten houses. He speaks:

"Oh no, Laude. You must walk with me. My good boy, there's
still time, but you can only choose one way.   Did you
know, every night I dig your grave deeper with a spoon?"

# Color of the Sun

From the parking lot, he watched his wife cross the street, and then traded waves as she mouthed goodbye before disappearing into the bright red, green, and gold Healthy Nation Cooperative. He loved to watch her walk. She still had that bounce, off to spread love and joy to those fine, young dreadheaded champions steadfastly laboring in the name of locally grown organic nutrition, seed-saving, and community centrality. What a place. What a life. What is it, anyway? He imagined her striding through the aisles, turning the lights on wherever she gazed. Our Lady of Kombucha. Compelling green eyes and amber hair. She'd be back in ten minutes, and the entire place will want to return to college, stop taking recreational drugs, commit to a career, find a soulmate and repopulate the planet.

She was a dazzling Kohinoor diamond–the rarest jewel. He shook his head: how did this happen? This world.

The western setting sun through the trees was equally dazzling, and the warmth and light on his face made him slide back into the Scandinavian lumbar support of the driver's seat and close his eyes. There were so many issues.

There was the young woman from his writing class who had gotten beaten up by her boyfriend, and the inner-city Ralph Ellison who needed a father. That afternoon he had told each that writing was an act of courage. With your writing, you can kick the teeth out of a monster. With your writing, you don't have to talk to the floor. He wanted to say just one thing to bring them up. He had tried–just one thing full of wisdom and truth, one thing that would turn the world over.

Of course, there were other issues. He had just read a recent study suggesting that 90% of the time, students thought about food and sex. At that rate, he had their attention for seven or eight minutes out of every class. So if teaching is indeed like planting corn, as the ancient Cherokee suggest, the crows are scarfing nine kernels out of ten. Regardless, tomorrow he would speak with his students concerning their community service project. They could give blood. They could give money. They could even, at his wife's suggestion, sponsor a teddy bear for a family with a child, or perhaps even a number of bears for a number of children. There were choices: there were  policeman bears and fireman bears. His students could choose and therefore impact, writing a personalized note to the bear's recipient.

"You could coach your young writers," his wife had told him. "You know, there are words."

He knew. He had agreed. 'Dear Young Man,' or 'Young Miss' it might say, or 'Dear Children,' or it might say something else, something else entirely, something perfect and beautiful, so perfect and beautiful you could even hold it in your hands. Regardless, he could already feel the impact, and he would speak with the Dean concerning how longitudinal community service impacts freshman attrition. He imagined sitting wing tip to wing tip with the man, deep in the correlation of blood, bears, and dropouts.

He would also appeal to the trustees for more money for the literary magazine. He saw himself standing tall in front of them, at ease, compassionate even, watching their faces shine and smile as he spoke. "What our students are accomplishing with their own writing will blaze the road ahead for this institution. They are taking the literary vanguard and elevating our academic community and our city. I am here today to ask for your support. I urge you: please give them an opportunity to rise, and rise they will." This world. He winced into the radiant heat for the greater good. This world.

And in the blur of the greater good, the issues, the Dean, and the magazine, the dreadlocks and kombucha,  he never heard the footsteps approaching the open window. He didn't hear anything until he felt the muzzle of the gun against his left ear—and then the disembodied voice.

"Keep your eyes shut, Mr.Man, and give me your wallet. Give me a problem, and I'll blow your head off. Do we have an understanding?"

The orders were clear and simple. There were two things to do. It would be so easy, he almost felt glad to do it. Just two things: yes, he understood that his eyes must remain closed–and of course, the money. He had no trouble with either request, and for goodness sake, he often gave away money. This was really no different, and as the beautiful light through the trees played on his face, he had no trouble passing his wallet along. Besides, he had just two things to do, and there was, of course, a very clear consequence. For example, it was made very clear what would happen if he didn't do one or both requests, and he had seen the peripheral outcome of such a thing on television as a child–those grizzly bear hunters in an alpine wilderness practicing with their sidearms and bravado. Their mission was apparently sheer audacity: to drop a nine foot, 1,000 pound mad-charging griz with a .45 revolver. He remembered a runt of a man saying, "Why, the good Lord made some men big and some men small, but Colonel Colt made us all equal." He also remembered how, in preparation for the hunt, the runt shot at plastic jugs of water, and the water geysering in all directions, a July 4th of water rooster tailing thirty feet into the air, and now, thirty years later, he saw it again instantly replay. And how ironic: with his closed eyes, he saw it–and then the sharp pain in his ear, wince, trickle of wetness.

"Have you received my message?"

He reassured the voice that he had received the message and that all was well. He reached down into his back left pocket and discovered, with great pleasure, that the wallet was still there. In one motion he passed it along and felt it, very gently, taken from his hand–and then the grumbling, the language, the low incomprehensible grumble and snarl.

"You don't seem to understand. I need some money."

There were just two things he had to do. He had done one, and now, for the life of him, he couldn't remember the second. He couldn't remember what it was. Instead, he saw his wife's face, who at this very moment was choosing a small dark chocolate dessert surprise and stocking up on organic field-grown tomatoes with the twenty-seven dollars he had given her. She was also going to pick up some locally produced mozzarella and basil. She wanted to make a simple Caprese salad for dinner. She had asked to borrow the money.

"What do you mean 'borrow'? We've bought two houses together. We've bought cars together. We've sent two girls to prestigious liberal arts institutions, only to have them return summa cum laude. We've bought 100 count Egyptian cotton sheets, couches, Tibetan rugs, Victorian standing lamps, toilet paper, studded snow tires. We've bought hepa-vacuum cleaners, plane tickets to destination weddings, replacement windows and doors. And while we're at it, dinners for two, three, four—the entire extended family, including their bar bill, tickets to *Rigoletto, Romeo and Juliet*, Isaac Pearlman, Stéphane Grapelli, the Boston Ballet at Tanglewood, and now you want to 'borrow' just a few dollars."

"Yes," she told him. "Yes, the twenty-seven dollars is probably going to do it, but now you're broke. There's nothing left. I'd take your credit card, but it's MIA. Where is your card?"

"Broke is not the word. We are merely bent, my love. Our friends at the bank will magically replenish the coffers, and we will, once again, walk the boulevards hand in hand with our heads held high."

She had laughed and taken the twenty-seven dollars. He always delighted in it: how he could make her laugh, and how her laugh would explode across her face and shake her body—a truly dazzling laugh. Yes. Without doubt, hers was the laughter of a very old soul.

Again the cool muzzle punched against his ear, and the brilliant light through the trees danced on his closed eyes. He thought that the word that could describe him would be forlorn, or baleful, perhaps disengaged, or disoriented. Maybe he was a combination of words. There might even be several combinations. Was he balefully disengaged? Forlornly disoriented? He recalled the Dean's sailing story that he had heard his first year at the college. Dismasted with engine trouble, dead in the water in a fifty knot gale, seven miles off Provincetown, bobbing in the shipping lanes, the

Coast Guard's radioman asked "Sir, What's your position?" And the Dean, a man who without question inhabited his own world said, "Why, I'm the Vice President of Academic Affairs, the Dean of Undergraduate Faculty, and the Roger H. Perry Professor of Humanities."

Already he could imagine telling the Dean his story, and the Dean, who loved Moliere and laughter, would lean in his chair, throw his head back and make some ribald reference to the body's reaction to fear.

"Almost soil those pants, Old Boy?"

"As a matter of fact, my entire suit is now in the hands of Gadue's Environmental Dry Cleaning."

Both would wretch out laughs, and the Dean would make that little rattle in his throat like a car with a dead battery in the middle of winter in the blue-black cold. But now, let's 'have some clarification, he thought. Let's have someone say whatever it is again, a little louder this time, maybe so it would rise above the sound of his own breathing and the low baritone grumbling in the air outside his window, air that smelled like honeysuckle, like the honeysuckle evenings of his Pennsylvania childhood. There was an evening of river fog so thick it could cut a man in half, and a mockingbird that sang for hours, jumping fence posts, doing a cardinal, a whip-poor-will, jaybird, redwing blackbird, pheasant, even the spring on his friend Alan's screen door. They sat in a field of fireflies watching the moon rise, heat lightning, and laughed out loud at that bird all night wondering what it was like to be in love with the world.

The next day they threw hay, racing a building storm that looked like a growing black anvil, and by evening, when every bale was stacked in the sweat and spinning green chaff, the sky let loose, and they went howling out in it, standing under the broken downspout of the barn, rolling in the puddles, both of them shouting, "We're filthy rich. Solid gold. Pennies from heaven."

But now you could spend your pennies on bears. You could order a policeman bear or a fireman bear. Mother bears were also available, astronaut bears, doctor bears, Count Dracula bears, Santa bears, and his personal favorite, the I'm

Crazy-About -You bear dressed in a white straight jacket with a front-centered big red heart. It was the Crazy Bear that he planned to gift  his wife on her summer birthday. He had placed the order earlier that day while she was out weeding her John Cabot roses. He had even created the attached note on the spot: "Darling, This crazy bear doesn't even come close to the way I feel about you." And what could be better? The teddy bear company would deliver your bear with a personalized note on the prearranged day. But they only wanted the first name, for anonymity's sake, for protection, privacy, for safety. Because strange things happen. Strange things have happened, and they will happen again. Yes, that's a good idea. After he gave the representative woman on the phone his credit card number, he thanked her for all she did.

"No worries," she said. "It's like I was sent to earth to help. We at Vermont Bear make the world a little brighter every day. And a very well-said note, by the way. You certainly know what to say."

No, he thought. No. His friend Alan always knew what to say, and Alan knew how to listen to the world. The next night, after the rain, they went back to the knoll and watched the moon rise, hoping the mocker would do it all over again, encore, but nothing doing, silence, only the sound of a distant truck on a gravel road.

"It wouldn't be fair to everyone else. You only get to hear music like that once in your life," Alan had told him. Still, even now, he could hear that bird between his ears, and he could see the heat lightning, fireflies, rising moon. He could smell the honeysuckle, and then there was the pain in his temple, voice like metal grinding on metal shoving him sideways.

"Where's your credit card? Answer me. Use words."

Yes, where is that credit card? Oh boy. He must have left it on the side table by the phone when he ordered the bear. Better grab it, he thought. I'll grab it as soon as I get home. Need to cover tracks. That woman can put two and two together.

"Answer me."

He could hear something click, like a door opening, or perhaps closing, and then hundreds of doors, their texture and sound opened and closed around him, separating warm and cold, dark and light, boy and man, hello and good-bye. So many doors. I had no idea, he thought. The depth and breadth of it all.

He heard something click.

What is it? What is it? Then it came to him. He could see: words coming across a long expanse of flat, dark water, all the right words, words in the right order. Blue words. Rippled. He could feel the words on his face, and he imagined the way the words expand and go out to the world after they're spoken. They're like those little cupids, he thought. Words are like those little cupids in Raphael paintings shooting arrows into the eyes of lovers, lovers who are already three-quarters the way out of their clothes.

He turned to his left and opened his eyes.

"I must have left the credit card by the . . . ."

And then the flash, and the flash had a sound. It struck like lightning, the brightest light finding its way through the trees, a glowing balloon of light with a smiley face blanketing everything around him, warm on his cheeks, hot even, in brilliant articulation, definition, explicit, to the point, dazzling, right to the point. You could put your finger right on it. Bold. Radiating. What was it? It was there, all around him. In all ten directions. Everywhere he looked. He was inside it. Spectacular. Everything was the color of the sun.

# How to Walk on the Sky

Scratch all good dogs behind their ears, and make
promises to the misunderstood remainder. Dance

the Grizzly Bear. Grizzly Bear like there's no
tomorrow. Repeat. Repeat. Evaluate your life

in lark factor. Go out larking. Lark every
day. Give away your sacred objects
and irreplaceable family heirlooms. Let

everybody borrow the truck. Donate
to lost causes. Stop brushing your hair.

Pray to St. Anthony while running up-hill
singing in Portuguese. Be forever

changing your mind. Drink enormous
quantities of green juice and then spit

in the faces of bastards and bitches. Play
the fiddle. Play the fiddle on one foot

shouting hound dog, arms assiduously
winging in the breeze, chrome grill

grin, unswerving, resolute, climbing
10,000 stairs, out there with the Jay

Birds, flapping, strutting on the great
foggy cumulous highway. Focus. Imagine

waving in ten directions. Wave. Keep
waving, and be sure to make yourself

at home. I'll be up there waiting for you.

# The Strange Disappearance of Peter January
## (and His Dancing Dog, Ellie)

I sit here and see him arriving all over again–the day after a three day blow–three days where the wind was so strong, it could take the skin off your face,  and then morning fog rose off a flat sea, and the sky became clear and bright. Even now, after years have gone by, I can see him stepping off our ferry, the Laura B.,  as I scrub the deck of my boat, and maybe it was his fiddle, or his little black dog, Ellie, or his fabulously wild red hair–it doesn't matter now–but I knew there was something about him, and sure enough, ever since he set foot on our island, we will never be the same.

His name was Peter January, and he came to play at our dances, tell us stories about good triumphing over evil–and fill the holes in his heart, he said. He said he wanted to live in a place where each second was his own, and time could be slowed down to a waltz, and then he'd play his waltz, and his little dog, Ellie, would jump back on her hind feet, barking and swaying to the music as she always did, and if you didn't have the luck to find a partner, you'd just dance alone.

He stayed with us all that summer, and when summer came to an end, he stayed on. He told us he had finally come home–and we were delighted, of course. A fiddler and a story-teller. He and Ellie would pack our dances, our children would run to them when they would meet them on the road, and our island filled with music and words for the first time in anyone's memory.

It was nearly October when he moved out of the hotel and took over the abandoned life-saving station on the seaward headlands. The place had been empty for years, and there wasn't much left to it, really. Most of the windows were blown out of the tower, and the doors were hanging off their hinges. Black-backed gulls had taken over the boathouse, the ancient sailing dory gone derelict,  the yard gone to wild roses, but in three weeks time, Peter had rebuilt the chimney with the round sea bricks storms would wash up from smashed lobster traps, and he made the doors snug and tight again with driftwood and line. He dug out the well and replaced every blown off shake on the place–went through bundles of the things. He re-windowed the tower, and painted every piece of trim bright white. He plastered the holes in the ceilings,  made a leather gasket out of an old boot, and got the kitchen hand pump going. I can still see him smile, the clank and squeal of it,  the rush of water tumbling out into the deep slate sink. In a few short weeks, the new red roof was gleaming in the sun, and you could see it  miles out to sea, hear a fiddle playing, and see Ellie dancing around the clipped yard. It was as if Peter had always lived there, the place seemed to fit him so well, or he it. No one could say.

It was that first fall that I taught him to fish. We patched up his wreck of a double-ended dory–laid a new gunwale on her, new pine tar and caulk, a few coats of paint, patched up her sails, and she was smart and trim–a black hull with ivory gunwales. She looked like she was levitating on the water, and Peter was a natural for all of it, and in a few short weeks, he could catch more cod on a long line than I could, and he became a dependable stern man during the winter lobstering season. He was handy and strong, and he'd whistle tunes all day to keep us hopeful–and that's what it did.

We had the greatest season of my life that winter, and I thought the three of us would work together all our lives, but that was before the dolphins arrived.

We were rounding the headlands not far from Peter's place when Ellie started jumping straight up in the air, barking at both of us, pleading with us it seemed, and that's when we saw them on the bow wave–three white-side dolphins–a huge male we thought. The second largest had to be the mother, and one quite a bit smaller swam at her side. They were following us for nearly an hour before we saw the baby tucked up and close to the mother's belly.

Peter could barely contain himself, ran forward, and lay face down on the bow, and when we stopped to check a trap, the dolphins would circle the boat, chattering and whistling at us, and although I had spent my life on the water, I had seen nothing compared to this show.

They stayed with us all afternoon, and by the time we were heading home, it seemed Peter had become a part of the family. He called the big male, Henry. He called  the mother, the Queen. Scooter was the name he began to call the small dolphin, and he called the baby dolphin, Daisy. And with each chirp and whistle, Peter would give a long winded explanation of what they had said. It was like they had plenty to talk about, plenty to discuss, and they talked about it most of the way back to the harbor–until all four vanished just as quickly as they had come.

The dolphins met us every day after that until the end of the season, arriving out of nowhere with an announcement from Ellie, and all concerned, man, dog, and dolphins reveled in each other's company.

At the end of the season, Peter left my boat and took his double-ender long-lining. It was disappointing for me. It's hard to find someone you enjoy working with, and I was hoping Peter would join me to go after swordfish, but that was not to be. I'd run into him, of course, and always ask about the white-sides, and he always kept me posted. He said Henry would talk to him for hours, and the Queen was shy at first, but had become very conversational, and the girls were characters, he said.

Soon everyone in town was filled with dolphin stories, but no one else had seen them except me, and just about everyone was asking if it was true: could Peter really talk to them? And I would tell them that the dolphins would speak dolphin, and Peter would speak Peter, but one night at a dance I was corrected. When the crowd was taking a break, Peter played a tune he called "A Conversation with Daisy" and then we all knew the truth. For a few minutes, all the music of the deep came pouring into the town hall, and the whole town stood there like they had never heard such a thing in their lives, which they hadn't, by the way.

Peter and Ellie fished by themselves all that summer and into the fall, and they did well–always enough to sell and get by. They got by just fine. They even planted a garden out at the windward house and had more beans, squash, and corn than anyone could use. They sold some and gave some away, and set up drying racks in the sun. By first frost they had enough for the whole winter ahead, and it was a real pleasure to stroll into Peter's kitchen and see all the jars stacked on the shelves, dried mint and basil hanging from the ceiling.

One night when he invited me out to dinner, and as we sat watching the light coming down, Peter told me he had finally found a homeland that he would never leave, and when I listened to him and looked out on the water as he spoke, I thought I knew what he was talking about, but now after all these years have gone by, I realize I had no idea.

It was almost the lobster season when it happened, and Peter and I had been working for weeks to get ready. He was going to be my stern man again, and I was very much looking forward to the camaraderie and the good times. The days had already gone cold, spitting snow and blustery. We were going to meet down at the dock early the next morning to make final preparations for opening day, but we ended up meeting a little sooner than we had planned.

Almost a month would go by before Peter was able to tell me what took place that afternoon. He told me he had his fishing anchor out when it happened. He was long-lining and doing well, and then his anchor line went slack, then tugged tight, and he could feel himself moving. He moved forward to reset it–thinking he was adrift, but it wouldn't budge. He even tried rowing out of it. That's when Henry surfaced and shrieked at him, and then the Queen and Scooter. The whole family was there–everyone except Daisy, and that's when he realized something was not right.

For the next three hours Henry pulled him, and he could see the bay and barrier islands fall away and disappear. A little fog came in and then a white-out snow squall–and then nothing on all horizons until he could see waves breaking over a rocky crag of a ledge.  When he got closer, it didn't take him long to figure it out. Somehow Daisy had gotten herself tangled in a gill net and was either going to drown or get thrashed to death by the waves. She was out there, helpless, stuck on the ledge.

Peter was over the side before he knew what happened and was cutting away at the net between rollers before he noticed Ellie out there with him, grabbing loose pieces of net in her teeth and pulling them off Daisy. He told me it wasn't a complicated thing: it was easy, in fact. They had her out in less than a minute, and they didn't even think about freezing until they were back in their dory.

Peter told me he could remember pulling his boots back on, and his shirt and jacket, and he could remember pulling Ellie out of the water, holding her close as he wrapped the sail around them, but the rest was all dream: the blowing snow, the dory magically getting underway again, his feet and hands and legs going numb, and then nothing.

I was about a mile off the island testing my engines when I first spotted them coming towards me, and I couldn't believe the sight–the double ender making way against the wind and tide, the frozen man and dog wrapped in the sail, and the huge dolphin's chatter and whistle. When I pulled them out of the boat, ice had totally encrusted them, but as I lifted Peter aboard, I could see him smile, and Ellie let out a long sigh.

Both of them lay near death for nearly a month when we heard the fiddle playing and went to his room to find Peter up on his feet and dressed, and the little dog, Ellie, barking and wagging her tail to greet us. Peter was full of smiles and good cheer, and ravenously hungry. I watched him eat most of a blueberry pie while he told me where he had been–Pangea, he said, where people we think are drowned go, living down there, he said. He said that the dolphins had taken him in, and he learned to speak their language, and while I looked at him, all the chirps and whistles of the ocean came out of his mouth.

It wasn't like he had changed after that; it was like we had changed, like we couldn't quite see him the way we had. He still played for our dances, and Ellie was still a favorite with us all, but it got harder and harder to speak with him and look at him full in the face knowing where his mind had taken him.

The times, of course, go on, and the way it goes Peter's swim became old news, someone's adventure at sea on an island known for its adventures–that is until the winter hurricane of that year. It took the island at spring tide, and with the storm surge, we saw water where we had never seen it before. The storm took the ferry dock and some fish houses, and one summer cottage along the harbor beach. Once, during the height, we even saw one wave roll down Main Street, and we lost a few boats and some shakes off our houses, but nobody was really hurt until we thought of Peter on the seaward side of the island.

When we got there, water was still a foot deep in what was left of the house. The sea had taken the old boat house and much of the boardwalk, and not a window was left unbroken in the tower. The front door had been ripped off its hinges, and the rooms were filled with seaweed and shell, Peter's broken canning jars, and not a trace of Peter or Ellie.

By April of that year we had nearly cleaned up the island and put everything back in place. We had a service for Peter and Ellie, and gave them a stone in the cemetery. He was drifting into our memories and into the anticipation of summer when he came walking into town with the dog–his clothes wet and torn, sea tangle and shells in his hair, and his big smile on his face, of course. Our people gathered around him, some of the men and women crying, children jubilant, and a few recoiling in fear. It was all the same for Peter, though–glad to see us, he said. Happy to be back. So we fed him soup, coffee, and pie, and we sat around him, and sat at his feet, and he told us how the dolphins saved him that night, how old Henry came in with the first storm surge and took him to Pangea, where he had been ever since–until this day. "You see, time is different there," he said. "A day can be short as a breath, or as long as a month. And there's peace there. Deep and serene. Like nothing in this world."

He was well dried-out when he left, and Ellie looked especially good after getting brushed by the kids, and with everyone reeling in the miracle of it all, we never thought it would be the last time we'd see him. After coming through so much, how could he not return, but it has been three years now since he walked away and took the path to his house.

The town decided to keep Peter's stone at the cemetery, and our children tend it well. They have planted sea roses over the empty grave, surrounded it with periwinkle shells, and someone has carved the figure of a dancing dog into the soft marble. Still, some of our people insist Peter and Ellie will return one of these days, hungry and worn out with big grins, and others claim he was drowned in the storm, and some say we lost him when he saved the young dolphin, and I suppose everyone is right in their own way, but I must tell you, sometimes before dawn when I round the seaward headlands on the way to my traps and pass what's left of his house, I think I can hear a fiddle singing high and lovely above my engines, and I imagine I even see them in the darkness on the rocks just above the breaking surf–a little black dog and a red-haired man, and I wave to them and give them a shout–my best–and sometimes I think I can hear barking and someone shouting back something that sounds an awful lot like my name.

## Star of the American Road

Without our realizing it, he had become
an old man–going blind and restless, always
dreaming and looking for something he couldn't
describe. His face and hands were wrinkled as if
the veins and capillaries were about to break
through his skin, as if somehow he had gotten
a line and a crease for every
step he had taken in life. His wife had died
years before, and his children had grown up and moved
away; still, he was never alone. He loved
children and children loved him, and there was often
an entourage of little people and their
dogs and cats–following him everywhere
he went. Whenever they were close, you could
hear them all–the shouting, barking, meowing–
and the old man's easy laugh. This
was a way you could tell him apart
from everyone–his laugh, and of course, his
perpetual smile. Everyone always said this was why
it happened to him when he was traveling
alone in the high plains desert.

So one day he left us to visit family
way off in the west, said
good-bye to the children and their
dogs and cats, and there was a little
crying. The dogs whined, and the cats
rubbed against his legs, but the old man

only smiled, as he so often did, patted each
head, rubbed each belly, and assured them all he'd
come back soon. Everyone watched him as he walked
away, and everyone was amazed at how
easily he could cover ground with his
heavy pack. It was true he was an old
man, but he was still very strong and agile, and before
long he was a speck in the distance.

He walked fast those first several days and covered
much ground, and sometimes he felt as though he were
floating above the rocks and grasses–floating
above the brush as he walked along. After several
weeks of hard going, he entered
a country that was new to him, but he had
exhausted himself and had become feverish, so he
made a camp in the blackness, built a fire
out of sweet grass and sage brush, and sat
inside the smoke for a white until he felt
strong again. And when he felt
strong again, they came for him.

It was easy and graceful the way the three
women appeared out of the smoke, and although
the old man was quite surprised, he
welcomed them, threw some dry wood into
the center of his circle of stones, and gave them
the last of his dried bread and tea. The four
ate dried bread and drank tea in a circle, and the old
man asked the women about the beautiful

desolate country, and they told him
everything they knew about the jagged
hills and barren valleys until the old man
felt as if he had lived there his whole
life, as if he had know the women forever.

It was then the three strangers told the old man
they were  the Wind, Fire, and Darkness, and that they
wanted something of him. Such an odd
thing to say, thought the man, but as he
looked closer into their faces, he could
see it was true. The woman who called
herself the Wind blew her words in a great
gentle rush of breath; there was a soft red
glow around the face and eyes of the woman who
called herself Fire; and the old man could see–
for the first time through the smoke–that the woman
who called herself Darkness had no
face at all. For a long time he
listened to what the three proposed, and he
found himself nodding, smiling occasionally, his easy
laugh returning like the chorus of a song.

Finally, he agreed to their proposal, and stood
up and shook their hands, and when
he touched them, the Wind made his hair
stand on end and made him feel
weightless in the breeze; the Fire warmed
his heart like he had never felt before, and his
body egan to give off a brilliant blue-white

glow; and the Darkness entered his half-blind eyes until
he could see into miles and miles of endless night.

It was in this way he began to rise from the earth. He
rose from the earth with his easy
smile and laugh, and waved good-bye to his three
new friends. He rose until his giant glow became
the small speck of light we now see when we're
traveling late, and we lose our way. You see, now
when we are traveling late and we lose
our way, we just have to ask the star, and the Wind
will tell us which way to go, or when the bone deep
cold comes upon us, all we have to do is
look to the star, and a warmth will come out of the very
center of our hearts, or when the night
envelopes us, all we have to do is
think of the light in the sky, and we can
see into the very bottom of darkness.

In the east, many people believe this man's name
was Omeka, and that he also had the power to shape-
change and speak the languages of all
animals. and in the south, people call him
Stone because of his perpetual endurance and boundless
strength, but as a small boy, I was told the old
man was known as Strong Heart, and this I
believe to be true, and this is how
Strong Heart left his body in the beautiful desolate
jagged hills of the Wind, Fire, and Darkness, and how he
became the Star of the American Road.

# Fastest Around the Ring

What you have to realize is that the girl's
eleven, and her grandfather is eighty-two.

You have to realize that by midnight, dirt
and smoke unite under mercury vapor lights
giving every lost and righteous soul
in Patrick Henry County a halo. By midnight

every sober and drunk denizen has
commingled, eaten his or her weight in dust
and chili dogs, and is leaning against the top
rail, waiting to see if Scarlett Ward and her
blue-black stud, Haley's Comet, will out-ride
the hoot and holler boys from Danville
–or the celebrated Charlotte Moraine Huntley
of Chatham, Virginia–the seat of gentility–
whose sons and daughters still manage to use
the word, Chancellorville, sometime
during the evening at every horse show.

And you have to realize that three years from now
during the state championship, some people in this
very crowd will see Haley slip and roll on the final
turn.
      The horse rolled, and there was a crack
of bones. Everybody heard it. The horse
rolled, leaving Scarlett lying in the dirt
to the accompaniment of shrieks and moans–red

lights of the ambulance
disappearing with her rag doll body.

                     Some people
in this very crowd will see her grandfather
take a baseball bat to Haley's head while it is
deep in a bucket of grain. They'll see the old man
drop him with one blow, spit on the carcass, and then
turn quietly to call the meat man.

You also have to realize the obvious: tonight
there's no contest, never was. Scarlet sits
quiet on the dozing Haley, whose head looks
more like a five gallon bucket than anything
out of the animal kingdom–that is
until they enter the ring–until her grandfather
smiles and gives her a nod–and she's
blue-black smoke, little girl well forward, talking
on the withers, talking to him whispering
in his ear.

                    "What's she saying, Howard?"
                    "You ask her," her grandfather says. "All
                    eggs and ham that horse is. I mean his
                    eyes are like two fried eggs, and his
                    moth so wide it could hold a Virginia
                    honey-smoke ham."

There's a gasp, somebody shouts when Haley's hind end
slides wide.

                I saw it
                        in the red dust and whirl

the grandfather's grin, the little girl and her red
pigtails flying across the finish line
                                        timekeeper
shaking his head, Rebel yells, bug-eyed–confirming
what everybody already knows.


She was blue-black smoke. I saw her. It was over
                        just like that.


But tonight, what you have to realize is easy: Scarlet
Ward is eleven. Her grandfather is eighty-two.
It's the year she is fastest around the ring.

# The Shrimp Business

"But in a story, which is a kind of dreaming, the dead sometimes smile and sit up and return to the world."

—Tim O'Brien

This is how I make it happen. Sometimes I imagine the title is up on a marquee, black letters on glowing white. Sometimes I imagine I queue-up in front of a silver ticket booth and go through the entire process. There's money, there's some shuffling,  there's an obese red haired boy pouring liquid butter on a nest of popcorn, an ancient Portuguese man dressed in black ushers me to a seat right as the lights go down. He whispers "Si Deus quiser." A thin ray of light cuts through the dark air and spreads across the scene, and oh my god, there we all are again. The camera pans in. I can see everything.

In the evening firelight, my mother's tears are transformed into molten gold, and I have no doubt that at this moment, if anyone touched her cheek, their fingers would recoil with third degree burns.  This, believe it or not, is a great improvement from this morning when she flatly refused to come to breakfast and announced that she wasn't "feeling herself." Hours later when she finally wanders down and takes a front and center seat at the hearth in her cat scratched Louis XIV Fauteuil armchair that we moved down from our museum attic last night, she manages a slight smile, and for good reason. My brother Jake is wearing the ridiculous lofty 18th century white pleated French chef's hat, an original *Toque Blanche*,  he found in our attic last year, and it puts an exclamation mark on his bean pole 6'4" frame.

The combination creates no clearance in our old French farmhouse: he has to bend over double to walk through any doorway, but he won't be suffering long. Our mother's birthday is the only day he'll take off his Stanford University baseball hat that's usually glued to his head. She smiles briefly at me, too. I'm wearing my standard coon skin cap. She says that I must have modeled for the Andrew Wyeth painting *Faraway*.

"You look exactly like that dreamy boy sitting in the grass." She winces, and shakes her head side to side, not in disapproval: she's just stating a fact.

Jake can't resist, and stands up straight with his hands behind his back. I can read his face. He's tipping his pitch. He's going to throw his four seam fastball that nobody can hit, and at seventeen, he  has a signed commitment from Dutch Fehring, the Stanford Indians' head coach, for a full ride scholarship. However, this four seamer is metaphorical.

"That's exactly what he's been doing all morning, too, while I've been slaving away."

She throws her head back and snorts out a laugh, then wipes the tears off her face with the sleeve of her fuzzy black Merino wool robe. I take the moment to pass her a cup of Irish Breakfast tea in her favorite green mug.

"Somebody has to do the dreaming around here," I say.

Jake cracks a smile, and then tips his head towards the fire. I turn back to the glow,  focus on the birthday cooking business, and today business is booming. Jake and I told her that we'd prepare anything, and all she had to do was make a list. Three months ago she made a request for a hearth-cooked meal, and she created a menu all right. We have a simmering pot of patty pan soup suspended from the eighteenth century fireplace crane; a Dutch oven of Caribbean baked beans;  sourdough rye bread baking in the beehive oven; sweet potatoes, red cabbage, lightly steamed kale and rainbow chard from our garden; a delightful cold cucumber, green bean, and red onion salad almondine waiting in the fridge. And of course, on display at the center of our ancient French farmhouse kitchen table is a gorgeous baba au rhun, our mother's new favorite cake, ever since Jake found a mouse-ragged copy of *Le Repertoire De La Cuisine* right next to the *Toque Blanche*, last year. We'll do candles later this evening with song, we'll get the family string trio going with a little bit of Bach's "Air on the G String," and accompany the music with some home-made vanilla ice cream that Jake and I cranked into existence that is now deep in the freezer. We also have an entire young goose spinning on the chained rotisserie of our 18th century fireplace.  We "bought" the goose and an additional surprise for our mother from our organic farmer neighbor, Joey Klein, who, as Jake always points out, is the most realistic farmer in Maine.

"The man has no stiff upper lip. When you ask Joey how he is, he actually tells you, and it's usually not very good. When we bought the goose, Joey said he was running the outfit solo, and he felt like two pounds of poop in a one pound bag."

Jake has his cast iron fish grill resting above some low coals ready to roast the two 30" striped bass he had pulled out of the surf at Parson's Beach at 5:00 A.M.

All of it creates a sort of fog in the kitchen. It's not smokey–more like a lens. Everything is magnified, vibrating in the light. Nothing, no corner, not even a knife, has a sharp edge. Everything is rounded, nothing could possibly hurt, and all the pieces fit together like there are no parts. In this light, I would swear that everything, floor to ceiling, including the people between, is carved out of one giant piece of waxy clay.

"A couple of striped bass chose not to migrate south," Jake announced when he stepped out of our groaning '58 Willis utility truck, holding up two 30 inch stripers that looked like twins. "I could have brought back a freezer full if it wasn't for the fog. Where's Carl Sandburg when you need him? Fog is supposed to appear on little cat feet, right? This fog came in like a galloping gray lion. It looked like smoke was billowing out of the water. Horror movie fog."

That was around noon. By 6:00 P.M., the entire coast of Maine is in lock-down foghorn from Bar Harbour to the Isles of Shoals, which, of course, belong to the unfortunate state of New Hampshire, and our old house, The Hurrying Angel, the Normandy farmhouse our great, great, great, great grandfather Spencer Victor Wright brought back one board at a time in the 1790s, is once again in deep. The cops are telling everybody to stay off the roads,  The Portland airport is closed. All planes are grounded, and for good reason. You can see the hand in front of your face, but you can't see your feet. Our orange cat, King Fergus, goes to the door and asks to be let out, but when we open it, he looks into the swirling gray cloud soup, sniffs the air, and then rockets back into the kitchen. Wally Kinnan, our weatherman, has Maine's attention. His voice cracks over the radio.

"This is not our usual Maine fog, ladies and gentlemen. This is a very serious situation. Don't become a statistic. Don't leave your home and hearth unless it's an absolute emergency, and if you do, tie a rope around your waist and take a compass. We'll even experience a few rumbles of thunder before we're completely out of the woods."

After a few sips of tea, our mother tries to come to the surface. She sits up straight, subtle clear of throat, and I already know where we're going: fifth grade science class. A large fin appears on her back, wide sharp teeth appear in back of her smile. She's circling prey in the water.

"Boys, what are the six types of fog?

Jake looks up from the Toque Blanche that has decided to lean a little to the left.

"Radiation fog."

Our mother nods, but does not smile. "Please define."

Jake spreads two striper filets across the huge custom curly maple cutting board he glued together and goes light with our salt shaker, heavy on the pepper and lemon juice.

"Radiation fog is a very common type of fog throughout the United States. It is most prevalent during the fall and winter. It forms overnight as the air near the ground cools and stabilizes. When this cooling causes the air to reach saturation, fog will form."

Our mother nods but does not smile. She turns to me.

"Upslope fog," I say, dodging her eyes. It's the one we have at the Hurrying Angel most of the time. The sea breeze pushes air up the three hundred foot bluff, producing fog right in front of our windows. It's the one I grew up with. I think I could have reported on upslope fog when I was two, but there are four more, and I'm coming up empty.

She looks back at Jake, who shakes his head while patting down the goose with Rosemary and his signature garlic paste.

When she looks back at me, I walk across our creaky French parquet oak floor to the door and open it up.

"What kind of fog are you?" I say into the soup.

It does not win me any points. Our mother takes a deep breath.

"Well, let's see. In addition, there's evaporation fog, advection fog, freezing fog, and hail fog."

She almost smiles.

"So which are we experiencing today at the Hurrying Angel, Kittery, Maine.

I put my nose to the kitchen door glass.

"Looks like Sherlock Holmes fog from here." I open the door again and act like I can see something out there, and then do my "Hound of the Baskervilles" impression. It gets me nowhere. Jake looks up from the fish.

"I think we're experiencing a perfect storm of fog, Mom. With our chilly wind this morning over the relatively warm October 18th ocean, we're getting cold advection and the previously mentioned upslope."

Jake takes a second to stick his tongue out at me. She doesn't see it. He goes on.

"It's not cold enough for ice fog, but this morning, there was some radiation fog lifting off the water just prior to the arrival of this thick gray blanket. And if there is a thunderstorm involved, we could see some hail fog covering everything like a secret sauce, or in our case, a *Velouté Gras*."

Our mother releases her first genuine smile of the day. King Fergus jumps up into her lap, and in the firelight, she looks about eighteen. She looks like the young woman who won the state backstroke championship–and missed the 1948 Olympics by a whisper.

"Finally, someone is paying attention around here," she says, stroking the cat.

Right on cue, there's a roll of thunder. Jake turns to me and winks. Sometimes you just have to admit it: scholar, athlete, musician, and comedian, all rolled into one totally weird, savant kid. Outside the extended family, Jake rarely speaks to anybody. Around here, you can't shut him up. When Jake entered the Horace Mitchell Primary School at six years old, he was soon evaluated by the district school psychologist and labeled autistic. Our mother was called and was told that Jake needed a special education, but when she went to pick him up, she found him in the principal's office reading the copy of her *New Yorker* he had stuffed into his lunch box. When she asked him what the problem was, Jake just shrugged his shoulders and lifted his palmed hands into the air.

"The alphabet. Dick and Jane. Run spot run. That's the problem. And those men over there."

He pointed at the district psychologist and the principal, who were eating their lunches.

"Mom, these men don't know how to use a knife and fork. Additionally, they eat nothing but sugar and fat."

When our mother tells the story, she always shuts her eyes tight before she speaks.

"Both men had milk lips and were covered in ketchup and mayonnaise from eating tater tots with their fingers. The school psychologist spoke to me with his mouth full. He told me that he was very sorry to say that Jake had years of remedial work ahead of him. While he spoke, a thin line of mayo escaped from the corners of his mouth. From a distance, it looked like he had fangs."

As a result, Jake, for a pricey fee that our father did not appreciate,  went to Berwick Academy, where our mother teaches fifth grade. Now, at seventeen, he's headed for Stanford, he can throw a 90 MPH four seam fastball, play the viola, and make an extraordinary velvety roux.

Now, it's my turn to squeeze my eyes shut. When I open them,  Jake is right there in front of me, and so is my mother. In the flickering light, they're real as they can get. I just want to touch them, tap each of them on the back like I'm knocking on a door, and then watch that door open. I want to shout, "Hey. This is it. This is our last night together by the fire." I want to shout, "Can you hear me? In a couple of weeks Jake's going to die in an auto accident. They're going to pull him out of that Jeep truck without a mark on him, but he's going to be dead, and Mom, you won't make it to fifty. Get it? This is our final performance? The curtain's coming down on the string trio?" But I don't. I resist. Instead, I sit tight and watch the movie. I want to watch the fire glow off all of our faces all night. I imagine that I'm planted in the theater's first row with the huge screen in front of me, and for Christ's sake, I'm taking it. It's my movie, and I want to see it again, and again, and again.

Our  carved oak grandfather clock that Great, Great, Great, Great hustled back from Normandy in 1790 strikes 7:00 P.M. I look out the eastern window. On a clear night, you can see the lights of freighters and fishing boats, and to the southeast, the lights of Portsmouth, and with a telescope, the Isles of Shoals. Tonight, it's different. Tonight, we're the only people left in the world.

Our mother slowly scans the 18th century cooking hearth and shakes her head.

"Boys, we could feed a wedding party."

She tries to smile, but ends up taking the sleeve of her plush black robe and wiping the tears from her face,  her jaw goes anvil, and for a moment, I think she's going to spit into the fire.

"That rotten, no-good son-of-a-bitch. I will not come back from this. This time, I will not be turned around. I'm sorry, boys, we're leaving. I just can't do it anymore."

Her words hang in the air and get magnified along with everything else in our kitchen.

"The entire east coast might be in lockdown, but the phones are still working, aren't they?"

I walk over to the antediluvian black extinct reptile of a wall phone  we use, put the receiver to my ear, and hear a dial tone. I nod. Her eyes glitter in the firelight. She doesn't stop stroking the cat.

"And that steamy pile of nitrogenous matter can't bestir himself to call me on my birthday, can he?"

Jake is standing so tall his chef's hat is brushing against the massive oak beam that spans the hearth. His teeth are glowing in the firelight. Right now, no kidding, Jake could double for Jimmy Stewart in *It's a Wonderful Life*.

"I'm sure he's stranded in a cozy airport bar somewhere with a rumpled and bedraggled audience, well along with the "oses.""

We all pitch back laughing. The "0ses" became a family joke when Jake wrote a paper in eighth grade for his health class about the five stages of drinking. Initially, normal people start with jocose, then enter verbose. They're happy, talkative, charming. They empty out all their funny stories. Then, after considerable exposure, there's a turn in the road, and drinkers arrive at bellicose, lachrymose. They get mouthy, surly, and then start crying.  And then finally the drunk train arrives at comatose: all the lights go out.

Jake continues. He has the stage.

"But Bad Bob doesn't follow those rules. He takes a drink, and goes straight to shit head."

Our mother puffs out her cheeks and does her dragon laugh. My eyes get tangled in the  French parquet oak floor. It looks like it's moving. I feel like I need to sit down in the brown grass and wrap my arms around my bent knees–just like the boy in *Faraway*.

I try to do the math, and this is what I calculate: since I was in first grade, she went to work two times with sunglasses to hide black eyes; four bruised cheeks from roundhouse slaps, one chipped tooth, two smashed Louis XV chairs waiting in our museum attic for some genius craftsperson to reassemble, and the spectacular cookout incident of last summer. After our neighbors went home, after a paradisiacal evening of pot luck and extended community hide and seek right out of a Norman Rockwell painting, he threatened her with the iron spatula we use for the grill, waving it over her head. His screaming was cut short, however. From a good sixty feet away, Jake nailed him with the hardball he always carries in his pocket. Jake's splitter took him in the solar plexus, and the three of us watched Bad Bob slowly melt on our front stone terrace that looks out to sea. Jake reached down,  picked up his baseball, grinned, and gave me a wink.

"'What a world, what a world.'" And then he did his Wicked Witch of the West laugh.

We left Bad Bob right there on the grass, his pink shirt  and seersucker blue pants glowing in the moonlight, and he laid there all night. We went inside and ate the rest of the strawberry-peach ice cream we had made for the party by the fire, Jake's and my mother's laughter punctuating the conversation, ringing like little silver bells.

I try to add them all up. There were others, too, and any one of them would have been enough to pack the bags, but she draws the line at a phone call, and no hang dog apology, no promise of a trip, no bouquet of yellow roses or box of dark chocolate can bring her back. There are a lot of things I don't understand, and I get to add this one to the list.

"So where are we headed?" I ask, and then look out the eastern windows into the inside-of-a-horse darkness. In the silence that follows, we can hear a ship's fog horn.

"Boys, hang on to your hats."

She pauses, her eyes darting from Jake to me and back again, still stroking King Fergus. Jake raises his southpaw arm and slides his fingers into the tight crack between the top of his *Toque Blanche*, and the oak carrier beam. I put both hands on top of my coonskin, hurricane style. Our mother nods. Her eyes flash in the firelight. Her wide smile is somewhere between DaVinci and Andy Warhole's Marilyn Monroe.

"Boys, we're going into the shrimp business."

I hear it like I'm standing at the bottom of a well. We get volition, direction, and destination all at the same time. Our maternal grandmother, Grandma Ola, lives in Lafayette, Louisiana, and the couple times we visited, we had the time of our lives. They are all Cajun French, and they live and die by "Laissez les bon temps rouler." Our father hates them, and the feeling is mutual.

The floor's moving a little. I have to sit down on my 18th century iron fireplace stool, but first I put my hands on the seat to make sure it's not too hot. I learn everything the hard way.

"How is this going to work?" I speak to the fire.

Jake looks at me and shakes his head slowly, side to side, takes a deep breath, and then shakes again.

"My pathetic young friend, this is how it's going to work. We're going to start with etouffee, seafood broil, move on to po' boys, jambalaya, gumbo, maque choux, and of course, shrimp stuffed alligator."

With each dish, my mother's smile grows wider. Jake can't stop.

"We'll then proceed to shrimp provencal, cognac shrimp with blanc sauce, shrimp scampi, and some Marseille-style shrimp stew."

I sit looking at the fire with both hands on my coon skin cap and smile. The shrimp business also means the Coes, my grandmother's Louisiana family, and if the Coes aren't laughing, they are singing, and if they aren't singing, they're asleep or dead. How my grandparents met is one of my mother's favorite stories, and I see we're heading in that direction. She's giving us all the signs. She puts her face in her hands and starts laughing, she clears her throat, nestles in her Frenchy chair like she is the principal dancer of the *Ballet Comique de la Reyne,* looks at each of us full in the face and says, "I'm going to tell you a story I never want you to forget." She's been doing this since I was old enough to keep my head up, and after about nine hundred tellings, I don't think she has anything to worry about. She starts by pointing her finger at each of us and shaking it.

"Your Grandfather Victor Wright met your Grandmother Ola Coe during WWI, and it wasn't at a dance."

By the time I was five, I had developed perfect audience. I knew when to nod, shake my head, and respond to call.

"No. Unuh. Not at a dance," I say. Our mother's smile widens. Jake grins, keeps his eyes on the spinning goose and simmering beans. She goes on.

"At twenty-one, Victor is a newly commissioned Merchant Mariner, a third deck officer, sailing out of Boston on the tug *Perth Amboy.* On July 21, 1918, Victor's tug, the *Perth Amboy,* is towing three barges of passengers and coal off Orleans, MA, and comes under fire by a German sub, the U 156."

She pauses and waits for Jake.

"Rotten sons-of—bitches," he says with a snarl.

Our mother nods with her fifth grade teacher's face and goes on.

"The sub strafes the *Perth Amboy*, setting it afire, and panicking the passengers aboard the barges. The sailor manning the tug's Mark 22 3" 50 caliber at the bow is killed within seconds."

Jake jumps in like he's reading music for his viola.

"No matter. With the ship floundering and an inferno at his back, third mate Victor Wright jumps on the gun and fends off the sub, blasting the hell out of the conning tower, and sends the Huns packing."

My mother's shark eyes turn on me. I know what to do.

"With the *Amboy Perth* in full blaze, the young third mate wrestles the tug's life-boat off its mounting and pushes it overboard into the hands of drowning crew and passengers, thus saving the souls of all."

My mother nods, closes her eyes, and executes her theatrical grimace that accompanies this part of the story.

"With the tug engulfed in flames, our boy dashes aft and engages the tug's water cannon. Twenty minutes later the fire is out, but the young officer, badly burned, his legs full of shrapnel, collapses on the charred deck. On July 22, what is left of Victor makes it to the Chelsea Naval Hospital, where Grandma Ola is a newly stationed Navy nurse. Victor is quickly triaged, and he is not expected to last the night."

This is where she looks at me with her over-wide teacher eyes. Her fin has broken the surface of the water. She's circling.

"What are the three levels of WWI triage?"

I am able to respond instantaneously for once. Still, I look up at the ceiling as if it's just coming to me."

"The three T's. Trivial, treatable, and terrible."

She nods, momentarily satisfied.

"That's right, boys. They morphine him up and put him dead last on the triage, but when the nurses are serving lunch to the guys who could eat, in his delirium, Victor sits full upright and yells, 'Sub off port bow' grabs the salt shaker off a passing tray and throws it across the room. It explodes against the wall. When Ola goes to clean it up, she reads the signs like any Creole-Cajun girl can do."

I take the moment and stop her for a second. Now, at the nine hundredth and one time, I have received new information.

"What do you mean 'Creole-Cajun.' I thought the Coes were Cajun. Period."

Jake shakes his head and takes the break in the action to paint the goose with the garlic paste I made with the mortar and pestle under his direction. My mother goes fifth grade.

"Certainly you've noticed your grandmother's golden skin and wide nose?"

I immediately nod. I shrug my shoulders.

"So?"

"Do you remember seeing her in a bathing suit at Holly Beach, the Cajun Riviera, when you were seven years old?"

That was five years ago, but I can see everything. It's what I do.  I nod. Of course I remember. Grandma Ola was spunky and very round, and when she jumped into the water, Jake said it was going to cause coastal flooding. He said something about Archimedes,and when she ducked under the waves, he shouted out "Eureka."

Our mother exhales slowly and gives me her full x-ray fifth grade teacher eye contact.

"Creole refers to people of mixed European and Black descent, especially in the Caribbean. Many people of Creole descent can be found where the United States touches the Gulf of Mexico."

At first the information bounces off me, and then I get it: her legs were as golden as her face. Her color didn't come from the sun. And then there was her beautiful tight curled auburn hair on its way to white. I say it aloud.

"Well, wait a minute. If Grandma Ola's Creole, the rest of us are too. How did it happen?

My brother doesn't suffer the comment silently. He speaks like he's making an announcement to the entire town.

"Now I know what the expression 'Oh, Brother' means."

Our mother is far more patient. Her smile goes wide.

"Think about it. Regardless, your grandmother said it was clear as day on the spotless wooden hospital floor: the salt said that Victor was the boy she was going to marry, so she does what any well brought up Acadian would do. When she is alone with the paperwork, she puts Victor in the "treatable" list, and forges the Commander's signature. Victor goes to the surgeon instead of the meat wagon. In the pandemonium, nobody notices, but three days later, when Victor comes to the surface briefly, Ola is right there, sitting on the edge of his bed with her auburn hair, green eyes, and golden skin.

"'Are you an angel?'" he asks her. "'Am I in heaven?'"

"'No,'" she tells him. "'No, Victor Wright. I'm no angel.'"

We say the final sentence together, Greek Chorus style.

"'No, I'm Ola Coe, and I'm going to be your wife.'"

King Fergus turns his head upward as if our mother is speaking to him, stretches out his giant six-toed paws on our mother's black wool robe and kneads some bread for a moment. She strokes him head to tail, and he leans into it. When she takes a sip of her tea, the fire light begins to vibrate. Now, she looks like Grace Kelly from Hitchcock's *Rear Window*.

"Victor looks up at her like the cherubs from Raphael's Sistine Madonna.

And then she says the sheet right below his waist begins to rise."

This is the place in the story where Jake looks at me with his profound practiced bewildered fried-egg eyed face. He offers me his palms-up open hands, puts his forefinger to his lips, and then raises his hand like he's in class. Our mother laughs and strokes the cat.

"Yes, Jake. Question? Comment?"

Jake tries to be serious, but as he speaks, he bends over double, and the laughter pours out of his belly.

"Mom, I just want to bring to your attention that there's one guy in this room who's not catching the drift."

He points at me like Uncle Sam.

"Mom, this kid thinks Victor's got a red squirrel in the bed."

She sips her tea again and stares at me, and then points back at Jake.

"Better fill him in."

Jake nods and motions me with his basting brush to come closer. I stand up, lean over, and he whispers in my ear. He's right. Now it's time for my eyes to go fried egg. All this time, I never really took notice of the rising sheets.

"Well, really," I say. "Victor must have had considerable inner resources," and I get a laugh from both of them. Our mother goes on.

"And boys, your grandmother–she told me all of this when I was your age."

She makes profound full-eyed contact and stabs her forefinger at me.

"I was still playing Kick The Can."

Jake shakes his head, and then checks in on the sourdough rye. He looks deep into the oven and smiles.

"Grandma Ola certainly didn't spare you any details."

My mother continues like nothing was said.

"That's right boys. Your Grandma Ola said, 'The sheets rose a little, and then that man slipped back into dreamland with a foot-long smile on his face, and never for a moment tried to conceal his intentions. When he came to the next day, Victor proposed. I don't think there was a place on his body that didn't hurt. I told him, if you live, and if you're ever able to catch me, I'll be yours.'"

Our mother takes a sip of tea and looks at us narrow-eyed like we don't know where she's going, but I could sail over these waters in the pitch black fog and arrive at safe harbor.

Her smile fades for a moment, and then goes high beam.

"Ola said she never saw a man work so hard in all her life, and recovering from those burns was excruciating, but Victor never whimpered, never complained. He pulls himself up and down those hospital stairs, goes from crutches to two canes, to a single. Victor is still limping around the hospital when the war ends on November 11. Ola returns home not long afterwards, and before she leaves, Victor asks her, 'How am I going to live without you?'"

Jake starts laughing. This is his part.

"She tells him 'And all this time, I thought you were a smart man.'"

The fire glows on our mother. She closes her eyes. Her face turns forty-seven. She opens her eyes, and she's eighteen.

"On Christmas eve at 9:00 PM, there's a knock at the door at the Coe house in Lafayette. It's frighteningly cold for Louisiana. It's 39 degrees, blackout rain, and the wind's howling hard from the north. Your great grandfather Clyde Louisiana Coe opens the front door only to find…"

This is my part of the story, and I shout it out.

"A shivering half-drowned racoon in a Navy blue pea coat."

My brother can't help but laugh, and when he does, the top of his *Toque Blanche* brushes the ceiling. Our mother moves on.

"But my grandfather knows. He knows without anyone telling him. He pulls that limp racoon right out of the rain and gives him a long huge hug, and says, "Son, so glad to meet you. We've been waiting for you, wondering when you'd show up.'"

She takes a breath, looks at the fire, holds it for a moment, and then slowly exhales.

"Victor walks across those cyprus floorboards towards the fireplace where they were all sitting. The whole family was there in front of the fire. Your Great Uncles Leo and Clyde Jr, were there. They were young men then, and both already had their own shrimp boats. Every inch of your 6'2" great grandmother Delia was there, all of them at the hearth with a big pot of shrimp gumbo bubbling on the fireplace crane. Victor walks across that floor with his head high and  without a trace of a limp, and when Ola sees him, she jumps into his arms."

Our mother very ceremoniously drops her head, and then looks at Jake. He is ready.

"And that's how we all got where we are today. You see, Little Brother, there was a lot of fucking back then."

Our mother says his name with her teacher's voice, but then melts into giggles. She never stops stroking our enormous orange cat. Both of them close their eyes in unison, and lower their heads. When our mother nods, King Fergus looks like he's nodding, too. Jake takes his 18th century Damascus steel chef's knife and gives the goose a little poke, and the fat sizzles on the coals below. I glance up at our big eastern kitchen window where our telescope is mounted. When it's clear, from our three hundred foot bluff, you can spot ships a good twelve miles out, but tonight there's nothing on the other side of the window but black and fog horns, and I have no doubt that the black goes all the way to Portugal. My eyes follow the flickering. Our Hollywood fire continues to do its work. When our mother speaks, once again, she looks like Grace Kelly.

"Clyde and Leo are still working on the water, and their sons Beau and Belmont, who are my age, are working with them. Boys do you know that the Coes have their own brand of shrimp called "Cajun Girls"—named after your grandfather's boat?"

I didn't know any of this. The last time I saw Louisiana, I was seven years old, Jake was twelve, and everybody called us "*chere*". Our great grandmother Delia was still alive, and when she wasn't hugging us, Grandma Ola was.

From his curled position on my mother's lap, King Fergus spins his head backwards and looks up into my mother's face. She looks back into the cat's eyes.

"When your Grandfather Victor died, Ola had the Cajun Girls pulled up on dry dock and had her completely refurbished. She's deep green–the color of Ola's eyes, with an amber rail, the color of her hair. Victor painted her that way so that every time he was far off in the gulf, he was still with his wife. He said that when he held the wheel, he felt like he was holding Ola's hand. Boys, the Cajun Girls is in perfect shape. She's in mothballs, ready."

"Ready for what?" I ask.

"Ready for us to come back to Louisiana if we ever wanted to and take our place in the family business."

I look at the floor. It's moving in waves. It's a dog chasing its tail. Still, I'm able to ask the question.

"What does that mean, 'take our place in the family business.' What does that look like?"

The fire glows off her face. I can hear purring clear across the room.

"My uncles and cousins all struggle with anything on land. They're devine workers, skilled watermen, but without Grandma Ola's steel pen, they'd be penniless. Your grandmother is getting on and could certainly use some back-up. I can run Cajun Girls–the business; when Jake retires from his Hall-of-Fame career in the big leagues, he can executive chef Cajun Girls–the restaurant; and you… "

She sticks out her hand like she's trying to touch me.

"You. You're going to captain Cajun Girls, the shrimp boat."

I'm as close to the fire as you can get without getting cooked. Still, I start shivering. I look down at my hands. They're giant compared to other kids my age. Already, I can  see them locked on the wheel of the *Cajun Girls*, gliding through orange sunset water, my face and arms leather brown, wide straw hat, my wide trawl net spilling over with shrimp, or as Grandma Ola might say, spilling over with "a mess of shrimps."

Jake gives the goose another poke with his chef's knife. It goes right through. His announcement is loud enough to reach the Isle of Shoals lightkeeper.

"Ring the bells, dong the gongs, dinner's up. The goose is cooked."

I pitch my head back laughing. A second later the phone rings.

All of us don't make a move. Instead, we look out the big eastern window. We're not here anymore. We're swirling around out there in the black fog. We're southbound. All three of us are '*Laissez les bon temps rouler*.'"

Jake giant steps over and grabs the black reptile off the wall. He's got his strikeout face on. He almost shouts into the phone.

"What do you want?"

Jake listens, and while he listens his eyes widen, and his face slowly stretches into a grin. I grip the edges of my stool with two hands. I don't care what anyone has to say. We've turned the corner. We've shut the door. Nobody's going to reel us back in. I'm skippering the Cajun Girls, and Dracula can live alone in his castle.

Jake's eyes pan over to our mother who is still fixated somewhere out the eastern bay window. He shakes his head slowly, side to side.

"It's for you," he says.

But our mother's iron. She's a marble statue. Not even the fire makes a noise. Fergus jumps off her lap, she stands, pulls her black robe tighter, and then walks over to the phone with a faceful of glittering golden tears. The phone floats up to her ear.

"Hello?"

She actually asks a question, and then her face goes halogen high beam. Silver bell laugh. She tilts her head back and looks up at the cracked horsehair plaster ceiling.

"Joey Kline, so sweet of you to call on my birthday."

Both she and Jake vibrate in the firelight. Jake looks at me, doubles over in laughter, and then covers his mouth with the palm of his hand.

"You have no idea," he whispers.

How did he get so tall, I wonder? He slides the goose off the rotisserie spit onto a large blue Rouen platter and places it on our farmhouse table. It's steaming in the firelight. We silently decant the rest of the food onto 18th century ceramics, and Jake quickly positions each dish like he's Donetello. Our mother gives off a high pitched laugh.

"What have you been eating, Joey?"

She listens and wipes the tears off her face, shaking her head.

"Steak, cheddar cheese, and chocolate ice cream will definitely bring you to an unhappy place. Tonight, move on to green leafy vegetables drizzled with olive oil, and tomorrow will be a new day."

She listens, and vigorously points at the phone, does a spinning index finger around her free ear, and then plants her face into her free hand.

"You have my personal guarantee on the matter, and again, know how much I appreciate your best wishes."

She places the phone back on the cradle and wipes her face with both hands.

"Boys, I think if we were staying here, Joey Kline would become my best friend. No doubt."

When she sees the table, her golden tears reappear. Our mother spreads out her arms, and for a moment, in her long black wool robe, she looks like she's going to fly away.

"Boys, look at what you've done."

And it is quite a sight. Jake has a pair of two foot tapers in full flame at the center, and we have everything lined-up, steaming on 18th century French ceramics: goose, the apple stuffing, red cabbage, sweet potatoes, roasted chestnuts, the two stripers, our chilled cucumber salad, the breadboard is covered with a round of lofty sourdough, which is next to Caribbean molasses baked beans, the secret sauce boat–all of it. We fill our plates and take our places by the fire. Jake gives me a nod, and I fetch the *Alsace Grand Cru* Riesling that's hiding in the woodshed fridge. When our mother sees it, she squeals in delight, and then lazer-eyes both of us.

"How in the world did a twelve year old and a seventeen year old procure such a fine Alsatian wine?"

I don't say anything, and Jake puts on his cherub face.

"I found it along the side of the road, Mom. Someone must have thrown it out of a car."

She looks back at me and goes anvil jaw.

"Tell me."

I stuff some striped bass in my mouth, and hold up a finger while I slowly chew. Both of them are staring at me. Jake shakes his head, no. I take my time, I'm going for forty chews, hoping to be miraculously saved from squealing. Jake saves me.

"A friend helped us there, Mom. We needed something to cut the goose fat."

She giggles, and Jake fills up her favorite floral etched wine glass. She nods back at him, and he fills up one for each of us. We raise them into the vibrating fire light, all of us carved little pieces of clay.

She takes a small sip.

"Oh," she says.

She takes another.

"Spectacular. And please give Joey Kline my bottomless thanks."

I nod, wolfing down some more striper. Cherub Jake looks up from his plate.

"Mom, there's no better man in an emergency. But next week, Little Brother and I need to split three cords of wood at Summer's Gale. It's in the fine print."

Jake raises his glass and both of us follow. We exchange prolonged Caravaggio inspired Italian Renaissance eye contact.

"To JoAnn Wright."

Our mother adds, "*Laissez le bon temps rouler.*"

We toast, we reach over and clink glasses, and toast again, but of course, the good times do not roll, but time does.

Time rolls on and does its work, but that's another movie, and I'm not watching it.

I'm sticking with this one. Our laughter fills the kitchen, King Fergus has returned to my mother's lap, and the firelight shines off all of our faces. We'll chew every bite slowly. We'll sing. We'll cut the baba au rhum, and have it with Madagascar vanilla bean ice cream. My mother will get out her cello, Jake his viola, and I'll try my best to do what Bach wants me to do on the top part of "Air on the G String," and "Jesu, Joy of Man's Desiring." Afterwards, our mother will look like Jacqueline du Pré and will tell me, with a slight English accent, "You're getting there. You've been practicing. Much improved bow hand and intonation." And Jake, who will look like Jimmy Stewart, will say, "Mom, I don't know what you're talking about. Every time this kid plays violin, it hurts Johann's feelings," and we will all roll in laughter in the French Impressionistic light–and with good reason. We're on our way. Nothing can stop us. We're in the shrimp business.

# About the Author

At one time or another, J.C. Ellefson has made his living as a hired hand, a black-smith, an apprentice Rolls Royce mechanic, and a fiddler in an old-timey band. He has taught at Shanghai International Studies University, the Universidade Dos Acores, and at Champlain College, where he was Poet-In-Residence and chair of The Committee on Verbal Insurrection. He has published poetry and short fiction in magazines throughout the United States, Canada, Great Britain, France, and Japan.  He and his wife, Lesley Wright, own and operate Summer's Gale Farm in Leicester, VT.

**More Odd Birds from Fomite...**

Fomite

www.ingramcontent.com/pod-product-compliance
Lightning Source LLC
Chambersburg PA
CBHW081026060726
47593CB00020B/2897